THE BLOSSOMS AND THE GREEN PHANTOM

The notice on the barn door said KEEP OUT—SECRET WORK GOING ON INSIDE, but still Junior Blossom's family hadn't tried to come in. Junior had just made the world's greatest secret invention, and his family didn't even care. If only he could get the Green Phantom off the ground, though, they would see that he was as great a Blossom as any of them. All it needed was one final, vital ingredient . . .

THE
BLOSSOMS
AND
THE GREEN
PHANTOM

Betsy Byars

A Lythway Book

CHIVERS PRESS
BATH

First published in Great Britain 1987
by
The Bodley Head Ltd
This Large Print edition published by
Chivers Press
by arrangement with
The Bodley Head Ltd
and in the U.S.A. with
Dell Publishing Co Inc
a division of
Bantam Doubleday Dell
Publishing Group
1989

ISBN 0 7451 0924 1

British Library Cataloguing in Publication Data

Byars, Betsy, *1928–*
The Blossoms and the green phantom
I. Title
813′.54 [J]

ISBN 0–7451–0924–1

For Olga,
with my thanks

THE GREEN PHANTOM

Junior stood in the doorway of the barn. All morning he had been working on his latest invention, and no one in the family had shown the slightest interest. At one point he had even put up a sign that said KEEP OUT—SECRET WORK GOING ON INSIDE, and still no one had tried to come in.

Junior shaded his eyes from the August sun and scanned the yard. It was as empty as it had been the last three times he came out.

The truck was gone, so Junior knew that Pap and Mud were off on their can-collecting rounds. Every Monday they went out and got cans from dumpsters and picnic areas. Pap sold the cans for five cents apiece. Sometimes they didn't get back until time for supper.

From the field behind the barn, Junior could hear the sounds of hooves on dry, packed earth—Sandy Boy. His sister, Maggie, was learning trick riding from their mom. This had been going on for two weeks, and neither of them cared about anything but becoming the first mother-daughter trick-riding team in the history of rodeo. They certainly didn't care about his invention.

Junior knew where every one in the family was but his brother, Vern. Vern went off somewhere every single afternoon and wouldn't tell anybody where he went.

Junior sighed. He turned and walked slowly back into the empty barn. It seemed to him that the family had separated, pulled apart like a ripe peach, and he had been dropped to the ground like the stone.

The thought was so sad it brought tears to his eyes. He brushed them away, leaving dirty streaks on his cheeks.

The sight of his invention perked him up. This was going to be the biggest, the best, and the most spectacular. His other inventions—his wings and his coyote trap—were nothing in comparison. This invention was so great that he got a patriotic feeling every time he looked at it.

And a lot of equipment had gone into this one. Junior had had to make a list for the first time in his life. He could say the list by heart now.

Garbage bags
String
Wire
Tape
Air mattresses
Patches for the air mattresses
Day-Glo paint (green)

After he had made the list he had written a word up in the top corner of the page, and then he had folded the corner down as if he were marking a page in a book. That was because this word was the secret ingredient, and if anybody saw what the secret ingredient was, they might be able to guess the invention.

Junior heard a noise outside, and he darted to the barn door. A bicycle had just turned onto their road. Maybe Vern was coming back early.

Junior raised his hand to shield his

eyes. No, it was Ralphie pedalling down the hill.

Junior was not sure whether he was glad to see Ralphie or not. It all depended on what mood Ralphie was in. Junior left the door slightly open behind him so Ralphie could catch a glimpse of the invention, which Junior had now given a name—the Green Phantom.

Junior had spent the last hour blowing up the Green Phantom with a bicycle pump. This was so that everyone could get the full effect of the Phantom's grandeur. Some of the air was leaking out now, however, and if someone didn't see it soon, the grandeur would be completely gone. Ralphie was better than nobody.

Junior pulled down his shirt as Ralphie got closer. He decided he would tell Ralphie the name of the invention, but he would not tell him what it was unless Ralphie absolutely insisted and promised not to—

Ralphie stopped his bicycle by pedalling backwards. He balanced for a moment beside Junior. Then he looked

4

worried and said, 'There's something on your head, Junior.'

Instantly distracted, Junior brushed his hand over his head. 'What? What is it?'

Ralphie said, 'Hair.'

Junior knew then that Ralphie was not going to be in a helpful mood. Still he stepped sideways so Ralphie could read his sign. Surely when Ralphie saw the words SECRET WORK GOING ON INSIDE, he would want to know what the secret work was.

Ralphie said, 'Is Maggie around?'

'She's down at the field with Mom. She's learning trick riding.' He turned back to his sign. 'Is the word *secret* spelt right?' he asked. 'Secret, you know, like something nobody can see.'

'*Secret* is, but *work's* spelt with a *u—w-U-r-k*.'

'It is not. We had that word in spelling. It's—'

Ralphie looked bored. 'Which field?'

Junior shoved the barn door all the way open, thereby revealing his secret invention for the first time to the public eye. It was, to Junior, like the moment

5

when an artist pulls a sheet off his masterpiece.

'You are probably wondering what that is,' he said to Ralphie.

'Nope,' Ralphie answered.

'All right!' Junior was getting desperate. 'I'll tell you its name, but not what it is. Its name is—'

Ralphie pushed off, and Junior's shoulders sagged as he watched Ralphie disappear around the barn.

Junior was once again alone. He went back into the barn. Now, for the first time, when he looked at his invention he did not get that patriotic feeling. The Phantom seemed to have shrunk.

Junior was instantly ashamed of himself. He told himself that nothing—not even the Statue of Liberty, for example, would look like much lying on the floor of a barn, particularly if the air was leaking out.

But, he went on, fill the Statue of Liberty with air and set it out on an island, and fill the Green Phantom and put it in the sky! Again patriotism flooded Junior's body.

From the field behind the barn came

6

a sharp cry from his sister as she fell off Sandy Boy. 'Did you hurt yourself, Maggie?' her mother called.

'No.'

'You want to rest awhile or keep going?'

'Keep going.'

'That's my girl.'

Junior heard Ralphie yell, 'Hey, can I come down?'

'Yes!' Maggie answered. 'I got something to show you!'

Now, Junior thought, it was going to be Maggie and Sandy Boy who were going to impress Ralphie, not him and the Phantom. And Maggie was impressive hanging off Sandy Boy upside down. Nobody could deny that. She was impressive even in her everyday clothes. When she got in white satin and spangles, she would be beautiful, but not as beautiful as . . . His eyes turned to the Green Phantom. He didn't need to finish the sentence.

'Just wait,' he said to the empty afternoon. 'I'll show them something really impressive. I'll show the whole wide world.'

7

To raise his spirits he began a new train of thought. Maybe at this very moment Pap was on his way home. Maybe Vern was too. Maybe Ralphie had told Maggie and his mom about the secret work and they were rushing up the hill. Maybe everyone would arrive at exactly the same moment and get to see the Green Phantom at exactly the same time.

Junior couldn't help himself. He smiled.

IN THE DUMPSTER

Pap was not on his way home. He was five miles away, standing in front of a garbage dumpster. His dog, Mud, was at his side. Both of them were listening.

'Something's alive in there, Mud,' Pap said.

Mud didn't need to be told. He had heard the faint scratching noises in the dumpster as soon as Pap had turned off the ignition of the truck.

He had jumped out of the window

8

like an arrow. He was now staring at the dumpster as intently as if he were trying to see through the metal. One front paw was raised. Mud's father had been a pointer.

'Didn't sound like a rat,' Pap went on. 'What do you think it was, Mud? Couldn't be a skunk or we'd smell it.'

Mud whined. His body trembled with excitement.

'What could it be?' Pap paused. He raised his voice. 'Possum?'

The word *possum* was always Pap's invitation to attack. Like, if Pap saw a hole in the ground, he'd point the toe of his boot at it and say, 'What's down there, Mud?' And Mud would wait and listen. Then Pap would say, 'Possum?' and Mud would know to start digging.

So when Mud heard Pap say, 'Possum,' at the dumpster, he put his feet up on the dumpster and began to dig at the metal. His high excited barks rang through the empty parking lot.

That was exactly what Pap had expected Mud to do. He would have been disappointed if Mud had done anything else. However, now that he

9

and Mud had had their little fun, he wanted to find out what was in the dumpster. He patted Mud on the head, smoothed the fur on his forehead.

'That's enough, Mud. Barking ain't going to do you any good. It ain't going to help whatever's in the dumpster either. Hush up and let's see if you scared it away.'

Mud stopped barking and planted his paws on the dumpster, but he could not stop his high excited whine. He had caught an animal smell, and he knew he was on the track of something.

Pap listened. The only sound from the dumpster was the drone of flies. Pap waited. Then, suddenly, he kicked the side of the dumpster with his boot. There was a frightened yelp from inside.

'Oh, I was afraid of that,' Pap said. He shook his head sadly.

Mud barked again. He had mistaken Pap's kick for another signal to attack. He began leaping up, trying to jump over the side of the dumpster.

Again Pap put his hand on Mud's head and smoothed his brow. 'Calm

10

down, calm down. It sounds like to me that one of your brothers is in there. I think it's a pup, Mud. I'm going to get my ladder.'

Pap had an aluminium folding ladder that he kept in the back of the truck for emergencies like this one. 'Yessir, I am afraid it is a pup, Mud.' He opened the ladder and set it on the ground. 'I don't like to think that somebody in this world of ours would be mean enough to throw a puppy in a dumpster like he was trash, but there's only one way to find out.'

As Pap put his foot on the first rung of the ladder, he wished for Vern. Vern was always the one to go up the ladder, to go into a dumpster, if necessary. Where was Vern anyway? Pap wondered. Vern had now missed two can-collection Mondays in a row.

'Catch me if I fall, Mud.' Mud wagged his tail, and Pap went up another step. He held on to the ladder with one hand, the dumpster with the other. The ladder trembled beneath his weight.

Mud came over to the ladder and

11

pawed the bottom rung. 'No, no, Mud, you wait down there.'

Pap knew Mud wanted to climb into the dumpster with him. Mud could climb wooden ladders, but his feet slid on aluminium. One time when Pap was still able to patch the roof, he had gone up the wooden extension ladder, and when he looked back, Mud was right behind him. Mud would have beaten Pap to the top if he could have passed him.

'You can't come with me today. I'll have to do the climbing for both of us.'

Pap peered into the dumpster. There was not much garbage—two brown sacks and a lot of loose stuff. He knew the puppy was in the far corner—that's where the yelp had come from—but he had to look hard to spot him.

The puppy had tried to hide in the garbage. Only his head was visible, but Pap figured that if the rest of the puppy was as miserable-looking as the head, the pup was in some trouble.

'Our fears were correct, Mud. Some miserable excuse for a person has put a puppy in here, and no telling how long he's been without food and water.'

He snapped his fingers and whistled. Mud whined at the bottom of the ladder and scratched the bottom rung. 'Not you,' Pap told him over his shoulder.

He leaned into the dumpster again. 'Come on, boy, come on over here. I'm not going to hurt you.'

The dog cringed in the far corner. His whole body was trembling. He tried to squirm deeper into the garbage. 'Come on, boy, come on.' Deep in the trash, the puppy's tail wagged with feeble hope.

'Oh, he ain't going to come, Mud. That's bad news. I got to go in after him.'

Pap hated to go into a dumpster. He never minded before his knees gave out, but Pap knew that a man with bad knees had no business in a dumpster. Still, once Pap had seen the skinny little brown-and-white spotted puppy down there in the garbage, cringing with fear and yet wagging his tail with hope, he had no choice.

'There ain't enough garbage for me

13

to climb out on, Mud, so I'm going to have to take the ladder over the top with me.' Pap had one foot over the edge of the dumpster now. 'This is a pitiful pup, just skin and bones. And he's got ticks on him, I can see them from here.'

He had one foot on the ladder and one over the dumpster. The position didn't feel right to Pap. 'This ain't going to work, Mud,' he said, but he was really talking to himself, working it out as he went. 'My other leg's better than this one. Well, anyway, this leg ain't going no higher. That's for sure.' He struggled with the knee.

'I'll put that one back down, and then I'll put this one over—No, Mud, it just plain ain't going to work. I'm going to have to go home for Junior or Vern. I'm coming down.'

At that moment, as his foot came over the top of the dumpster, he lost his balance. He pitched forward, leaning over the dumpster on his stomach, teetering on the edge. His foot that had been on the top of the ladder, kicked the ladder away. There was a yelp of pain from Mud.

Pap hung on the edge of the dumpster for thirty long, painful seconds. He was more in the dumpster than out, and he kicked with his feet, and tossed his head back, trying to throw his weight the other way. His whole body had become a terrible, awkward see-saw.

If he had to fall, which he knew he did, he wanted to fall to the ground rather than into the dumpster.

It was a losing battle. Pap knew it, and he looked down into the dumpster to see where he was going to land. That was bad. The bags of garbage were on the far side, just loose trash lay beneath him.

He made one last struggle to slide backwards to the ground, but he felt himself slipping the other way. His long yell of fright rang out and then echoed in the dumpster. There was a heavy thud, and silence.

Mud had run under the truck when the ladder struck him on the head. The ladder had hit him over the left eye, and the eye was bleeding. He blinked rapidly to clear it.

With his good eye, he looked at the place where Pap's old boots had disappeared. His brow was wrinkled. His ears were flat against his head.

After a moment Mud crawled out from under the truck. He walked towards the dumpster, cautiously circling the ladder. His tail was between his legs. His left eye was closed.

He barked once. There was no answer. Mud pawed the dumpster. He barked again.

This time when there was no answer, Mud began to whine. He moved around the parking lot in an uneven circle, whining and pausing occasionally to look at the dumpster.

Finally, Mud crawled under the truck. He lay down. Then he licked his front paw and began to draw it over his swollen, wounded eye.

THE BB GUN FRIEND

Vern was not on his way home either. He was one mile down the road at his friend Michael's house, and he was jumping up and down on bedsprings. He and Michael had pulled the bedsprings out from the storage shed to use as a trampoline. This had been Vern's idea.

'Let me have a turn,' Michael said at last.

'Sure,' Vern said quickly.

Vern bounced three more times, pretending he was having more fun than he was. Then he leapt off the springs and made a solid landing in the dust, arms out to his sides. It was, he thought, the way gymnasts landed after a perfect routine. He glanced at Michael to see if he was impressed. He did not appear to be. 'Your turn,' he said.

Vern sat with his back against the oak tree while Michael bounced up and down for a while. 'It's more fun if you do tricks,' Vern called.

Michael tried a sit-bounce without success. He didn't bounce back up. He tried a knee-bounce and cried, 'Ow!' He lumbered off the springs. 'That hurt,' he said.

He pulled up his jeans to examine his knees. 'Let's don't do this anymore,' he said.

'All right, let's shoot your BB gun,' Vern said quickly. 'I'll make a target and you get the—'

'I don't want to do that.'

'Come on.'

'No. We did that all day yesterday.'

To Vern, this was no reason not to do it again today. He felt he could happily have spent the rest of his life shooting Michael's BB gun.

'Let's ask your dad to let us shoot the rifle.'

'No, I don't want to.'

'Come on.'

'No!'

'Then let's get your fishing rod and go down to the creek.' Michael was the only person Vern knew who had a fishing rod, not a home-made fishing

18

pole—he had one of those himself. This was a fishing rod, with a reel and a fibreglass case.

'No, I'm tired of those things.'

Vern could not understand how Michael could ever become tired of a BB gun, a rifle, and a rod and reel, three things he would have given anything to own. Still, he did not want to lose a friend who had access to them. He said, 'What *do* you want to do?'

'You know.'

'What?'

'You know.'

'No, I don't.'

'I want to go to your house.'

Vern stopped breathing. He and Michael had been friends for exactly two weeks, by far the best two weeks of Vern's life. Michael was not only the first friend Vern had ever had, but he was the ideal friend. Michael lived the way boys were supposed to live, Vern thought, and owned the things boys were supposed to own, like BB guns. The one cloud on the two-week friendship was the fact that every now and then Michael said the very words he had just said, 'I want to go to your house.'

The reason Vern had made the bedspring trampoline in the first place was because he sensed Michael was once again about to make the suggestion. Now all that laboured jumping had been for nothing. The suggestion had come anyway.

Vern sighed. He did not want to take Michael home. He did not want Michael to see that he himself lived all wrong and owned nothing. He also did not want Michael to see his family, because Michael's family was different. Michael had two parents, a mother and a father, and the father—it was the father Vern really envied—did things with his children, like let them shoot his rifle.

'There's nothing to do there,' Vern said, kicking his foot in the dust.

'Well, there's nothing to do here either.'

Vern gaped at Michael. He wanted to list again all the pleasures—the BB gun, the rod and reel, the—

'Let's go,' Michael said.

Vern sensed from Michael's tone of voice that he was not going to be put off. He got slowly to his feet. He brushed off the seat of his pants.

'Mom,' Michael yelled, 'we're going to Vern's house.'

Michael's mom came to the door. Michael's family had only been living at the farm since June, and they had not met many neighbours. 'Where do you live, Vern?' she asked.

'About a mile down that way.'

'Are your folks at home?'

'My mom and my granddad and my brother and sister are. My dad's dead.'

'Oh, I'm sorry. I guess it'll be all right, Michael, but you be back by suppertime.'

'I will,' Michael called happily. He kicked the stand up on his bike. It was a ten-speed bike, the exact kind Vern would have chosen for himself.

Vern pulled his bike away from the tree trunk where it had been leaning. It was an old bike of his father's, so old it did not have a kickstand. Kickstands probably hadn't even been invented back then. It also had, to Vern's shame, balloon tyres.

With Michael in the lead, the two boys pedalled down the dusty drive. As Michael turned onto the main road, he stopped. 'Who's that?' he asked, astonishment in his voice and expression.

Vern stopped his bike beside Michael's. He looked down the road where Michael was pointing.

He swallowed. It was Mad Mary, and she was picking up a dead animal from the road. She examined it and, satisfied, tucked it into her shoulder bag.

'Who is that?' Michael asked again.

'Mad Mary,' Vern answered.

Mad Mary had been a friend of his grandfather's all his life. Now, ever since she had rescued Junior from the coyote trap, she had become a family friend. It was something else about his family he didn't want Michael to know.

'She eats things she finds on the road,' Vern explained, careful not to reveal too much. 'She lives in a cave.'

'Have you ever seen it?'

'From a distance. I didn't want to go

22

too close because of the vultures.'

'Vultures?'

'Yes. They roost over her cave.'

Michael looked at him with respect. 'You'll have to take me there sometime.' He hesitated. He nodded his head in Mary's direction. 'Is she dangerous?'

'She knows me. I better go first.'

'Thanks.'

With Vern in the lead, the boys pedalled down the road towards Mad Mary. She was on the left-hand side of the road now, striding along in her man's boots. Her long, crook-necked cane matched her stride.

As they passed her Vern raised his hand. 'Hi, Mary,' he said. Her head snapped up, and she looked at him with her bright, piercing eyes. 'Afternoon,' she said.

Vern leaned over his handlebars and began to pedal faster. He was relieved she had answered, yet disappointed she had not spoken his name.

ON SANDY BOY

'Come on down,' Maggie called to Ralphie. 'You can be my first audience.'

Maggie had never been happier in her life. Her happiness had begun two weeks ago when her mom had spoken that magic sentence, 'Maggie, I think you and me ought to get ourselves up a trick-riding, mother-daughter routine.'

They had been sitting at the kitchen table, across from each other. Maggie had been looking at her nails, wondering why they wouldn't grow.

Maggie had lifted her head, a quick bird-like movement. She thought she hadn't heard right.

'Are you serious, Vicki?' Pap asked.

Pap was at the sink cutting up fish for supper. He turned in surprise. Fish water dripped on the linoleum floor, but no one noticed.

'Yes, I am serious.' Vicki looked at Pap over Maggie's head. 'B.B. called me this morning. Thelma's out of the

24

Wranglers, and B.B. wants me back. It was B.B. who thought up the mother-daughter idea.'

At one time, when the Blossom children were small, the whole family had gone on the rodeo circuit. Vicki Blossom was a trick rider and performed with the Wrangler Riders between events. Pap, in his younger days, had done rope tricks. Cotton Blossom, the children's father, had been World's Champion Single Steer Roper.

Cotton Blossom had been killed by a steer in Ogallala, Nebraska. After that Pap and the kids stayed home on the Blossom farm, and Vicki went with the Wrangler Riders by herself.

'Maggie always has been a natural,' Vicki went on. 'She could stand up on a horse before she could stand up on the floor. When she was five years old she won first place in the barrel race in the Junior Rodeo.'

'I know that.'

'So what do you think?'

'Well,' Pap went on, 'I think it's up to Maggie, but if it's my opinion you want—'

'I do, Pap, we both do.'

'Well, she's a Blossom, and we Blossoms are known for doing what we set out to do. As I see it, it's up to her.'

Maggie had been sitting there hardly breathing while they talked about her. Her eyes had gotten larger and shinier. Before her mother could ask the question, she answered it. 'I want it more than anything in the world.'

'Then, go for it,' Pap said. 'I wouldn't mind getting back on the circuit myself.' He turned to the sink. 'I probably couldn't do nothing more than pick up pop cans from under the stands but . . .'

'Then it's settled!' Maggie's mom reached across the table and took Maggie's hands. She squeezed her daughter harder than Maggie could ever remember having been squeezed before.

This made Maggie brave enough to ask, 'Will I get to have a white satin shirt like the other Wranglers?'

'Shug, you'll have the shiniest white satin shirt of the bunch.'

Ever since that evening Maggie had not had one single moment of anything but pure happiness. Even when she fell off Sandy Boy and landed hard on the ground, even when she hurt herself, the happiness was still there inside, whole and unharmed.

*   *   *

While Ralphie coasted down the hill on his bike Maggie said to her mom, 'Here I go!'

Her mom slapped Sandy Boy on the flank. 'It's all yours.' Maggie dug her heels into the horse.

'Be careful,' Ralphie called as she started across the field. He couldn't help himself. He had never seen Maggie on a horse before. It worried him, not only because she seemed so careless about her safety but because, in some more troublesome way, he sensed she was about to ride out of his life.

Maggie turned in the saddle. 'Ralphie, trick riders can't be both good and careful. My mom told me that, and my mom's the best.'

Ralphie leaned on the seat of his bike and concentrated on not looking as stupid as he felt. His cheeks burned. The tips of his ears turned red. Maggie grinned and flung her braids over her shoulders.

A path had been worn into the grassy field, a wide oval where Maggie had been practising her trick riding. Maggie was riding fast. Ralphie wanted to ask if she was going too fast, but his ears were still burning from his last stupidity.

He threw a sideways glance at Mrs Blossom. She was obviously not worried. She beamed with pride as her eyes followed Maggie and Sandy Boy around the field.

Maggie paused at the far side of the field. 'Here I come!' she called. 'Only, Ralphie, try to imagine me with music and satin, shining like the sun!'

That would be easy for Ralphie. He had never imagined her any other way.

Again she dug her heels into Sandy Boy. She and Sandy Boy came around the circle fast. As Maggie passed in front of Ralphie and her mom, she hooked her knee in the saddle and dropped off the side of the horse.

Her arms, her braids were flung over her head. She was grinning. She was the most beautiful thing Ralphie had ever seen in his life.

Ralphie applauded.

JUNIOR'S WORDS

Junior lifted his head. He heard Maggie, Ralphie, and his mother coming up from the meadow. At last! Now they would see the Green Phantom. He could not wait for Pap and Vern.

He made a few adjustments on the sagging garbage bags and pulled the air mattresses into a circle. Every time he wasn't looking, the three air mattresses bunched up into a pyramid. 'Now, stay round like that,' he told them. He went outside the barn to wait.

He was standing there, smiling in anticipation, when his mother came around the barn. At that moment Junior heard her say something to

Maggie that caused the smile to freeze on his face, because the words his mother said to Maggie were the very words he had always wanted her to say to him.

And the painful thing was that up until this moment, Junior had not known how much he needed to hear these words. He had not even known these words existed. And to hear his words said to someone else . . .

The words his mother had said to Maggie were, 'Oh, love, your dad would be so proud of you.'

'What?' Junior said. The word came out sharply, as if someone had struck him on the back.

His mom smiled and hugged Maggie. 'I was just telling Maggie how proud your dad would be of her.'

The words went to Junior's heart like a knife. Every single day since his father had died four years ago, Junior had missed his father, every single night his father had visited Junior in his dreams and rubbed his hand over Junior's head the way he used to do, 'For luck.' Every single rainy afternoon

Junior had taken out the old snapshots of his father and gone over them with a magnifying glass, but Junior had never once thought of trying to make his father proud.

Junior's pink face paled. He had not even realized his father could be made proud. He felt cheated. All this time he could have—

Junior's thoughts broke off with the terrible realization that he had done nothing his father could be proud of. Every one of his inventions had failed.

Last summer he had made himself wings, the best wings he could possibly make. The only place he had gone was twenty feet straight down.

The horror continued. Last month he had made the best coyote trap he could possibly make. Only he had not trapped a coyote. He had trapped two members of his own family.

And if his dad had seen both of those failures—and Junior was pretty sure now that he had—then his dad would be the opposite of proud. And Junior knew his opposites. The opposite of proud was ashamed.

'Junior, you look pale,' his mother said. She let go of Maggie's shoulders and came over to him. 'Are you all right?'

'Not really,' he said. He was breathing through his mouth. His lips were pale, too, and dry. His blood pounded in his ears. His chest ached.

She put her hand on his forehead. 'You don't have any fever.'

'It's worse than fever,' he muttered through his parched lips.

'What do you have? Is it your stomach?'

Junior shook his head. Tears filled his eyes. He put one hand over his heart.

'You have a pain in your chest?'

He shook his head. He turned one finger inward to point to the centre of his chest.

'Your heart?'

'What kind of pain?'

He shook his head. It was the kind of thing that could never be told. If everyone knew that his father was ashamed of him, then they would be ashamed of him too.

'Junior.' His mother looked into his eyes. He turned his head away.

'Junior!'

Then a dam broke inside him. He couldn't help himself. He told.

'Dad's ashamed of me.' He began crying. It was like an explosion. His chest heaved with sobs. He couldn't get them out fast enough. He could barely speak.

'Everything I do fails.' He gasped for breath. 'I'm a terrible, terrible failure.' He began making little hand movements as if he was reaching for something. 'Every single Blossom—' He tried swallowing back the sobs, but that didn't work either. 'Every single Blossom is a success but me.' He gasped again. 'I can't do anything right.' He put out his hands to show that he had tried his best and had still come up empty. 'I've never done anything right.' Now came the worst of all. 'And I never will!'

He gave up trying to continue and put his hands over his face. Instantly his mother's arms were around him. This was the only place Junior had ever liked to be when he was crying, but even her arms couldn't help him today.

'Junior!' she cried. She kissed him on top of the head again and again. 'You are not a failure. You're not a failure at all. You are a wonderful, wonderful boy.'

He shook his head against her.

'The whole family is proud of you.' She paused to hug him harder and rain more kisses on the top of his head. 'You are just'—more kisses and tight hugs—'wonderful! You are the sweetest, kindest, most lovable boy in the world. We all love you very much, don't we, everybody? You are a wonderful, wonderful boy!'

'No, I'm not,' he said, his voice muffled against her body. The unspilt sobs formed a solid knot of pain in his chest.

'You are too! Now, look at me.' She turned up his tear-streaked face. 'This isn't like you at all, Junior. I want you to tell me what is wrong.'

He raised his hands again and let them fall. The word 'Everything' burst from his lips.

34

'Everything is not wrong. Now, calm down and start at the beginning. No, don't turn your head away. Look at me. What has happened?'

He made a sweeping gesture in the direction of the barn where his invention lay in the dust. He saw it through his tears. It looked so pitiful, he put his hands over his eyes. All of the air had now leaked out of the garbage bags, and the air mattresses were back in a triangle.

'Are you talking about your invention?'

Junior nodded, and then he shook his head because the word *invention* was too grand to use in connection with the pile of junk in the barn.

His mother turned slightly so she could look into the barn. 'What is it, Junior?'

'See, you can't tell.'

He burst into tears again. He couldn't help it. He felt as if he were going to be spending the rest of his life trying to get rid of the terrible sobs stuck in his chest.

'Now, stop it, Junior. I mean it. Stop

it!'

'I'm trying.'

'Stop it this minute. You can't keep this up. You are going to make yourself sick. Now, have you got control of yourself?'

He nodded.

'Then tell me what that thing in the barn is. I have a right to know. I demand to know.'

When his mother spoke in that voice, he knew he had to answer.

'It is'—he paused to correct himself—'it was supposed to be a flying saucer.'

A BLOSSOM PROMISE

Vern and Michael were pedalling their bikes down the hill to the Blossom farm. Vern could see as soon as they crossed Snake Creek that his family was involved in some sort of crisis. They were in a tense cluster in front of the barn.

36

Vern's spirits sank. He coasted through the pine trees. Blackbirds flew up, filling the air with the beating of wings and loud cries. When the calls of the blackbirds had faded into the distance, Vern heard a new, more troublesome sound—Junior's sobs. Then Vern knew that, as usual, the family crisis involved Junior.

'Hold it a minute,' he told Michael.

Vern paused and got off his bike. He pretended to examine his bicycle chain; what he was really examining was his family.

The situation had to be bad because Maggie was wiping her eyes with her braids, and his mother was hugging Junior and kissing the top of his head. The only dry eyes in the group, apparently, were Ralphie's, and Ralphie was looking down at the ground and shuffling his foot in the dust. Vern could see that Ralphie was uncomfortable, and Vern knew it took a lot to make Ralphie uncomfortable.

He glanced at his friend through the spokes of his bicycle wheel. Michael was watchng the Blossom family with interest. He had one hand up, shading his eyes.

'My brother must have hurt himself,' Vern told Michael. He jiggled the bicycle chain as if testing it.

'That's what I figured,' Michael said.

'My brother hurts himself a lot.'

'Mine too. He's accident-prone.'

Vern sighed with relief. At last he and Michael had something in common—accident-prone little brothers. Vern threw his leg over his bike and shoved off. 'I hope he wasn't trying to fly off the roof again.'

Michael paused to say, 'Your brother flew, *f-l-e-w*, flew off the roof?'

'Tried to.'

'Wow.'

Vern glanced at Michael as he pulled up beside him. He wasn't ready to add that Junior had landed at the feet of some policemen who had come to notify the family that Pap had been arrested. Michael had been impressed by Vern's friendship with Mad Mary and his brother's flight off the barn. That was miracle enough for one day.

Vern bent over his handlebars. He

38

had to pedal hard to get up the hill because his balloon tyres were low. Michael pulled ahead easily but waited for him on the crest of the hill.

Vern pushed his bike over to Maggie. 'What's going on?' he asked in a low voice.

Maggie wiped more tears on the ends of her braids. 'Junior thinks he's a failure.'

'Junior?'

She nodded.

'He's never thought that before.'

'Well, he does now.'

'What's he failed at?'

'Everything.'

'Like what?'

'Like his invention.' Maggie pointed to the air mattress-garbage bag invention, which could be seen through the barn door.

'That's his invention?'

'Yes.'

'He's invented air mattresses?'

Maggie shot him a look of such fury that he stepped back. He glanced at Michael to see if Michael thought he'd been stupid. Michael gave him a look of understanding. Vern realized he and Michael had big sisters in common too.

'It is a flying saucer,' Maggie announced.

'Oh, well. I guess that figures.' Vern turned to Michael. In a low voice he said, 'Usually his inventions look better than that. They don't always do what they're supposed to, but they look good. You should have seen his wings. They were neat.'

'Shh!' Maggie said.

Vicki Blossom was on her knees now, by Junior, wiping his tears on the hem of her shirt. 'Now,' she was saying, 'Junior Blossom, you get this through your head. You are not now, never have been, and never will be a failure.'

She paused to smooth his hair back from his face and straighten his clothes. Then she tucked his shirt-tail in. Every time she did one of these things, Junior felt a little better.

'You are not a failure and neither is your UFO. You are going to have the best flying saucer in the entire world. That is a promise—a promise from one Blossom to another.'

There was nothing in the world more binding than a Blossom promise. An awed stillness came over the Blossoms in the group.

Vicki Blossom got up. She turned Junior around and pulled him against her. They were facing Vern and Michael and Maggie and Ralphie. Then she made the promise even more binding.

'This boy,' she said, and she hugged Junior hard, 'this boy is going to have the most beautiful, the most wonderful, the most spectacular UFO the world has ever seen.'

BACK AT THE DUMPSTER

Pap came to his senses slowly. He was lying on his back in the dumpster. His head was propped up on one side, and his feet were propped up on the other. His arms were outstretched.

For a moment Pap didn't know where he was. He lay quietly, blinking his eyes open and shut on the unfamiliar sights in front of him. Then he remembered that sickening, cartwheel lunge that had sent him over the side of the dumpster. Remembering it made him dizzy all over again.

He moaned, 'I'm killed.' He closed his eyes in despair. 'And my neck's broke.'

Tears squeezed from his eyes. He lay for a moment, too miserable to move. Then, slowly, he put one hand to the back of his neck. He rubbed his spine gently to see how bad the break was. After a minute, he turned his head slightly from side to side.

'Well, my neck may not be broke,' he conceded, 'but my knees are. Bound to be.'

He pulled himself up into a sitting position, with his legs straight out in front of him. He looked at his aching knees for a while before he tried to bend them. He could feel them throbbing against the leg of his pants. He pulled his right leg up, then his left.

'Well, they still bend, but I know they ain't going to bear my weight.'

It took Pap five minutes to get to his

feet. Then he had a moment of dizziness so great, he had to sit down on one of the bags of garbage. He bent forward and hung his head between his swollen knees.

As soon as Mud heard Pap stirring around in the dumpster, he came out from under the truck. He gave that one questioning bark.

'I hear you,' Pap said weakly.

Mud barked again.

'I hear you! Let me get over this dizzy spell.'

Mud approached the dumpster slowly. He paused to figure out the situation. His head was turned to the side. He whined softly.

'Yes, I'm in here,' Pap said.

Suddenly, in a blaze of inspiration, Mud began to dig. Red dirt flew in an arc behind his back.

'That won't do no good,' Pap said. 'You can't tunnel through solid metal.' He turned his neck from side to side again, testing it.

Mud kept digging.

Pap raised his voice. 'I said that won't do no good, Mud. Quit it.'

Mud stopped digging and sat, his paws in the hole he had started. A good tunnel had been his only solution to the problem, and he waited for Pap to tell him what to do now.

Five minutes dragged by, ten. Flies began to buzz around Pap's head. He waved them away.

'Ain't nobody coming with some garbage?' he moaned. He lifted his head, clasped his hands over his chest. 'Please, please, somebody come with some garbage.'

There was a noise in the corner of the dumpster. Pap had forgotten about the puppy, and he looked around.

The puppy was there, watching Pap from his nest of trash. 'I can't coax you out,' Pap told it. 'I'm half killed.'

The puppy wagged its thin tail.

'I was going to call you Dump if I got you out of here,' Pap said.

Again the puppy wagged its tail, setting the garbage around him in motion.

'But there's no need to call you anything now. Plus, you're the one got me into this.'

Now the puppy's body went into motion. He squirmed with pleasure.

With one hand on his sore neck, Pap looked around. 'And the big trouble is that there ain't enough garbage in here. There was enough to break my fall, thank God, but not enough to climb out on.'

He sighed. 'Maybe somebody'll come along.' He batted a fly away from his face. 'The world changes, but one thing that don't change is garbage. People always have had garbage, and they always will, and sooner or later somebody'll decide to get rid of theirs, and you and me will get out of this mess.'

At that moment, Pap heard a car. He lifted his head. He couldn't believe it was true. 'They're here,' he said. He began to struggle to his feet. 'Somebody's already come!' He grabbed the top of the dumpster and pulled himself erect. His arms trembled with the effort.

He looked out of the dumpster for the first time since his fall. A car was there—a two-tone Buick—but it had

45

not pulled over by the dumpster. The car was parked just off the road.

Pap called, 'Hello! Hello!'

There were two people in the Buick, but neither one heard him. The windows were closed, and the engine was running.

Pap changed his call to 'Help! Help!'

Still they did not hear. The man and woman had pulled off the road, apparently, to finish an argument. He was yelling at her and she was yelling at him.

'People in the Buick! Hello! Hello!'

The fight continued. The man was slamming his fist against the steering wheel for emphasis. The woman was shaking her head.

Pap extended both arms over the side of the dumpster in a pleading gesture. 'Please, couple in the Buick, please, look where I'm at. Help me! Please!'

He began pounding his hands on the side of the dumpster. That got the woman's attention, and she turned and glanced out of the window. She was frowning, and even without the frown she would have been an ugly woman.

With it, she was the ugliest woman Pap had ever seen in his life.

'Please! Help me!' he begged her.

The woman kept frowning at him through the glass. Pap made a gesture begging her to roll down her window. She turned and said something to the man. To Pap's shock, the man began to drive off.

'Wait, wait! Oh, please don't leave me in this dumpster. Please don't go! Help!'

The Buick pulled onto the road. It disappeared around the bend, and the sound of the engine faded.

In the silence that followed, Pap rested his forehead against the rust-specked dumpster. He sighed deeply. After a long moment he turned and looked down at the bag of garbage he had been sitting on.

It had taken on the shape of Pap's body, like a beanbag chair. Pap sat down slowly. He took out his old handkerchief and wiped his eyes.

The banging on the side of the dumpster had sent the puppy deeper into the loose garbage, but now he started crawling out on his belly.

'Ugly women,' Pap told the puppy, 'never have cared for me.' He wiped his face again. 'And right now I don't care for them neither.'

THE SECRET INGREDIENT

Junior had never been on the receiving end of a Blossom promise before, and he had not realized how awesome it would be. Oh, he had always known that a Blossom promise was sacred, that it was the way knight's promises used to be. That was why he had always been very, very careful not to make one.

Like one time he had stood at the top of White Run Falls with an inflated garbage bag under each arm. Icy green water pulled at his feet. From the bank Vern had said, 'I'm tired of waiting. I don't think you're going over the falls. I don't think you've got the guts.'

'Oh, yes, I do,' Junior had answered.

'Blossom promise?' Vern had asked.

Junior would have given anything to have said with a sneer, 'Yes, Vern, Blossom promise,' but he knew that if he did, he would have to do it.

Even though the falls were a lot higher than he had thought, even though the rocks were a lot craggier and the water a lot colder, even though the garbage bags were leaking valuable air out under his arms, he would have had to go.

'Blossom promise?' Vern asked again.

Junior's lowered head was his answer. Vern had gotten up with a snort of disgust and started home. Later, Junior had folded up his shrunken garbage bags and followed.

The Blossom promise had made Junior stop crying completely, at least it made his eyes stop. His chest was still shaking with an occasional leftover sob every now and then. Every time Junior's body shuddered, his mom hugged him.

Vicki Blossom was now looking at Maggie and Ralphie and Vern and Michael over the top of Junior's head.

Although Junior could not see her expression, he knew from the length of the silence that it was a serious look.

When she finally spoke, her voice was serious too. 'You,' she said, and just the way she said it let Junior know every one of them better do what his mother said. 'You are going to help Junior with his flying saucer, do you understand me?'

Ralphie pointed to himself and raised his eyebrows.

'Yes, you too, Ralphie, Junior may need you. I'm including all of you.' She looked at Michael. 'I'm sorry, I don't know your name—'

'Michael,' Vern said quickly.

'Michael. Junior needs every single one of you. Now, Junior will be in charge tonight. I want that clearly understood. Junior is in charge, and you four will do whatever he tells you to do.'

If anybody other than a Blossom had said that to Ralphie, he would have answered, 'You aren't my boss,' but he acted differently when he was with Maggie and her family.

Junior's chest shuddered with what was to be his last sob. There was no reason to cry now. He had everything he wanted out of life. He could not have worked it out better if he had sat down with a pencil and a piece of paper.

He was in charge and they would do what he told them. His mother was wonderful at arranging things.

'This is Junior's UFO—'

'It's known as the Green Phantom,' Junior interrupted. Then as he saw them glance at the barn, he added quickly, 'Well, it's not green yet, but it will be when I spray paint it. I'm not going to do that till the last minute. Just before it goes up, I'm spraying it'—he paused for effect—'Day-Glo green.'

He could feel his mom nod. She rested her chin on the top of his head.

She said, 'The Green Phantom is, as of right this minute, the first priority in the Blossom family, is that understood?'

Everyone nodded.

'It is even more important, Maggie,

than our riding.'

'Yes'm.'

Then she said, 'Now what exactly do you need, Junior? You tell them what you want them to do.'

'I only need one thing. Everything else is done. I've wired the air mattresses together myself. I've tied the garbage bags where I want them. I've filled the whole thing up with air—I used the bicycle pump. That was just so I could see how it was going to look. Now I only need one thing.'

'What is it, Junior? Tell us and we'll get it.' It was Vern who spoke this time. Now that his mother had included Michael in the project, he figured they couldn't lose. After all, Michael and his family had every single thing there was in the world. Michael's father's workshop was like a hardware store. Michael's room was like the sporting goods department at Sears. 'If we don't have it, we can probably borrow it,' Vern said.

'It's only one thing, but it's a very, very, very important thing,' Junior said. This was the secret ingredient, the word so secret he had written it in the corner of his list and then turned the corner down.

'What?' Vern asked.

'You might not think of it as important, but it is very, very, very—'

'All right. We're begging,' Ralphie said. 'What is this thing that is so important?'

Junior felt that the moment was now right for his revelation. Everyone was ready. Everyone was waiting. One of them was even getting impatient.

Junior said the secret word. 'Helium.'

TICKS AND THINGS

Mud barked. This was a series of sharp barks, different from that single questioning bark he had given from time to time. Pap lumbered to his feet.

'What is it, Mud? You see something?' Pap peered over the side of the dumpster. 'I don't see nothing. What do you see? I—' Then he broke

53

off.

A jogger came around the bend in the road. Pap's heart leapt at the sight. 'Over here! Over here!' he shouted.

He beckoned the approaching jogger with both hands. As the jogger came into closer view, Pap frowned. The man had on earphones. He was wearing a Walkman.

Pap raised his voice and his arms. He waved his arms over his head.

'Help! Help! Help!'

The man did not glance in the direction of the dumpster. He kept running in rhythm, arms to this chest, a weight in each hand.

'Help! Look over here! Help!' Then Pap broke off and said the words Mud had been waiting for. 'Go get him, Mud! Go get him!'

In an instant, Mud was running for the road. He caught up with the jogger and began barking at his heels. The man turned and with one practised kick, caught Mud on the side on the head.

There was a loud yelp of pain.

Pap yelled, 'Mud, you all right?'

Mud came back into view slowly. He was shaking his head. He went directly under the truck. 'Mud?' Mud looked at Pap and shook his head again, trying to rid himself of the sharp pain in his ear.

Pap said, 'There ought to be a law against them earphones, and there ought to be another law against joggers kicking dogs. You all right, Mud?'

Mud rested his head on his paws. One eye was closed, and one ear pulled back in pain.

'Well, you tried. I thank you for that.'

Slowly, Pap sank onto his garbage bag chair. He reached down his hand to Dump. Pat had now been in the dumpster for so long that he and Dump were friends.

The friendship had come slowly, because it was Pap's way to let the dog make the first move. Pap would make conversation, but Dump had to come on his own. Finally, Dump had crawled out of his corner on his belly.

'Come if you want to, don't come if you don't,' was all Pap had said to him.

Before long Dump had been at Pap's

feet, and Pap had picked him up. When the jogger came by, he had been in Pap's lap, allowing Pap to pick ticks off his head.

'Let's see, Dump,' Pap said, taking Dump on his lap again, 'where were we—tick number nine, and I believe that's the last of them.'

Pap twisted Dump's ears around, checking for stray ticks. 'One more, baby tick. There. That's the lot.'

Pap scratched Dump behind the ears. Pap always knew where dogs like to be scratched. He got it right first time, every time. Mud liked to be scratched on his back, just above the tail. This was a behind-the-ears dog.

As Pap scratched, Dump lifted his hind leg and made scratching motions in the air.

'You're a nice little dog,' Pap said. 'Good dog.'

Outside the dumpster, Mud heard the words and it set his tail in motion too. It was instinct, however, not happiness that wagged Mud's tail. Mud was miserable. His eye hurt and his ear throbbed, but what hurt most was the knowledge that Pap had another dog in the dumpster. Mud gave one of those sharp single barks that urged, insisted actually, that Pap notice him.

'I'd help you if I could, Mud,' Pap said with a sigh. He kept scratching Dump.

A flea moved behind Mud's ear, and he scratched it without getting up. He just twisted slightly and scratched with his back paw. Then he rested his aching head back on his paws.

The cut over Mud's eye still stung. He had taken care of it the best he could by licking his paw and wiping the cut, but that was never as satisfactory as a direct lick. From time to time he still tried to shake off the pain in his ear.

There was another 'Good dog' from the dumpster, and Mud's tail made a low, unhappy sweep in the dust. He began to whine, and Pap called, 'Mud, you too. Good dog, Mud.'

Suddenly, Mud lifted his ears. He heard the sound of a motorcycle in the distance. He crawled out from under the truck.

'Somebody coming, Mud?'

There were sounds of another struggle and then Pap's face appeared over the side of the dumpster. He was holding on to the dumpster like a baby holding on to its crib.

Pap heard the motorcycle then. He knew it was useless, but he couldn't help himself. He began yelling, 'Help help help help help,' over and over.

There was something about this that Mud didn't like. He had known from the moment Pap disappeared into the dumpster that something was wrong, badly wrong, but he had not known how wrong until he heard the panic in Pap's voice. This was something Mud had never heard before. Pap was afraid.

Mud threw back his head and began to howl. He was a good strong howler, and now there were three noises in the air—Mud's howls, Pap's *helps*, and the drone of the motorcycle.

The motorcycle went by in a roar. The two riders never glanced at the dumpster. The noise of the motorcycle began to fade. Then it was gone.

Pap was the next to give up. His *helps* grew fainter and weaker, and then he sagged back into the garbage bag chair and was silent.

Mud kept howling. These were his howls of misery, and when Mud was really unhappy, he could howl for hours.

Dump pawed at Pap's leg, asking to get back in his lap. After a moment, Pap picked him up. 'There was two of them on the bike, Dump. Didn't neither one of them see me.'

He patted Dump with one hand. With the other, he pulled out his handkerchief and wiped his eyes.

THE HELIUM HERO

Everyone was just as impressed with his saying 'Helium' as Junior had hoped they would be.

'Yes, helium,' he said again with a firm nod.

Actually, it was more than just being impressed. They were shocked, Junior thought happily. Even his mother was standing there with her mouth open.

He knew this because he could feel her chin drop onto the top of his head.

Junior was delighted with their reaction. Everyone, seeing the unpainted air mattresses and the garbage bags, had probably thought that he, Junior, didn't know what he was doing, that this was just another of Junior's crazy inventions that wouldn't work. With one word, he had changed all that.

He couldn't help himself. He said the word one more time. 'Helium.'

It was Vern who stopped Junior from saying it any more. 'Helium!' He came two steps closer to his mom. 'Mom, we can't get helium!'

He felt he had to let her know this was completely impossible before she put him in charge of it. 'Helium costs money—big money—and it comes in heavy cans like—' Vern sputtered for words and couldn't find them. With his hands he measured out a large bomb-shaped object. 'You can't just go in a store and buy helium!'

Needing corroboration, he turned to the one person in the crowd he could count on. 'Can you, Michael?'

Michael shook his head.

Vern turned back to his mother. 'See, Mom?' he said.

The disbelief of Vern and Michael, his mother's shocked chin resting on his head, did not worry Junior at all. He had expected this reaction. He would have been disappointed if it had been any other way.

He admitted to himself that a half-hour ago these reactions might have sent him into another of those terrible crying fits. Not now. Anyway, he didn't want to cry again for a long, long time. His eyes were still stinging from the last cry, and his nose was still swollen shut. If at all possible, Junior wanted to avoid crying for the rest of his life.

The difference was that Junior was now secure. He had become a Blossom promise, and that included even helium.

Vern looked around for help. 'Talk to him, Maggie.'

Maggie felt terrible. She desperately wanted to help Junior. The sight of

Junior crying because he was a failure had touched her deeply. It had caught her in the middle of feeling both happy and successful, selfishly happy and successful, it seemed now, and she would have done anything, anything to help Junior get the garbage bags and air mattresses airborne.

Now she was faced with the truth. She could not help Junior. None of them could. She avoided Junior's hopeful smile.

'Mom, it's true,' she said, misery in her face and voice. 'I don't even think you can get it. Maybe you even have to have a prescription. I don't think ordinary people are allowed to have helium.'

There was a moment of silence. Every single person had now stated that helium was the most rare, the most impossible-to-obtain element in the world. This was exactly the moment Ralphie had been waiting for.

'I can get it,' he said.

Junior drew in his breath with surprise, then he smiled. He should have known all along it would be

Ralphie. Ralphie specialized in the impossible. Junior would never forget that wonderful moment in the hospital when Ralphie had accomplished the impossible for the first time.

Junior and Ralphie had been in side-by-side hospital beds. Junior was there because he had fallen off the barn roof and broken both his legs. Ralphie had fallen off a riding lawn mower three years earlier and cut his leg off, and now he was having another operation and getting a new artificial leg.

Junior had been desperate. Maggie was going to the court-house for Pap's trial and she wouldn't take him.

'I can't, Junior,' she had said. 'Wheelchairs won't fit on the bus.'

Everything she said made Junior more desperate. At the absolute peak of his desperation, Ralphie spoke up. And Ralphie had said the most wonderful words Junior had ever heard. 'We could take a cab.'

One thing about Ralphie. He knew how to do the impossible and he knew how to do it with class. That had been the one and only cab ride of Junior's life, and he would remember it forever.

'Where would you get helium?' Vern asked with a slight emphasis on the word *you*. He felt his friend Michael had somehow been belittled. If Michael's family didn't have helium, nobody would.

'From my mom.'

'Your mother has helium?' Vicki Blossom asked.

Vicki Blossom was just coming out of the shock of hearing the word *helium* herself. She knew nothing about helium. She didn't even know if the word had one *l* or two, which she would have to find out before she could look it up in the Yellow Pages.

'Yes.'

'At your house?'

'Yes.'

'Your mom has helium?' She looked at him as if she thought he didn't know the meaning of the word.

'Yes.'

'Helium?'

'Yes, Mrs Blossom, helium!'

'What exactly does your mom do, Ralphie?'

As the questions and answers continued, Junior kept looking from Ralphie to his mom. It was like being at a tennis match.

'My mother,' Ralphie said, and from the way he said mother instead of mom, Junior knew Ralphie's mother was a very, very important person indeed. As usual Ralphie did not let Junior down.

'My mother owns the Balloonerie.'

A BUNCH OF HELIUM

Junior and Ralphie were in the barn, looking at the Green Phantom. Junior was beaming with pride, but Ralphie was not smiling.

'Of course, it's not sprayed with the Day-Glo paint yet,' Junior said. He began walking around the Phantom so he could enjoy it from every angle. As he went, he rearranged the air mattresses into a better circle. 'I just sprayed one tiny little dot—over here, see? Right there.' He pointed at the spot with a dirty finger. 'I wanted to

65

make sure it was green enough.'

'I don't think there's any question that it's green enough,' Ralphie said. Ralphie still had not smiled.

'I'm not going to spray the whole thing until it's full of helium because if I do it now, see there are some wrinkles here and here, and the Day-Glo won't get in the wrinkles. I want it to be perfect.'

'I'm sure you do,' Ralphie said. He put his hands in his pockets.

The Green Phantom was the least perfect thing Ralphie had ever seen in his life. On a scale of one to ten, it wasn't even a one. Patched air mattresses in a triangle with collapsing garbage bags on top—it was like the stuff his little brothers were always making, only his little brothers at least understood that the stuff they made was pitiful. They even had the good sense to be ashamed of it. 'Mom, Ralphie's spying on us,' they'd cry if he even came close. And they didn't expect their space junk to actually fly, they were happy just to sit in it and pretend to be flying.

Ralphie shook his head. The more he looked at the Phantom, as Junior insisted everyone call it, the more he realized that it was not going to take 'some helium' to fill the Phantom. It was going to take a whole bunch of helium.

Ralphie cleared his throat. 'Excuse me,' he said, 'but were you planning to fill the, er, air mattresses, or the garbage bags as well.'

'The whole thing,' Junior said happily. 'The works.'

Ralphie said, 'Mmm.'

'Why did you say that? Mmm.'

Ralphie could see that he had managed to get Junior worried. 'Junior, don't you know what happens to people who fill up both their mattresses and their garbage bags? Don't you read *Time* magazine?'

'No, no. We don't even take magazines.'

'I hate to be the one to break this to you, Junior, but people who fill up both their mattresses and their garbage bags float off and are never seen or heard from again. See, helium acts like a magnet, and you get too much of the stuff and it won't let go of you and—'

At that moment, Ralphie looked up and saw Maggie standing in the door of the barn. 'Is anything wrong?' she asked.

Junior said, 'I don't know. Ralphie says helium acts like a magnet and if I put too much inside, it will pull me off with it.'

Maggie smiled. 'Junior, you know not to believe everything Ralphie says.'

Junior turned to Ralphie. 'But you weren't teasing when you said that your mom was the balloon lady, were you? She really does run the Balloonerie?'

'Yes, my mom runs the Balloonerie.'

'And you can get the helium?'

'I said I could, didn't I?'

'Junior,' Maggie said, 'you ought to know by now that when Ralphie says he can do something, it's so.'

Ralphie thought he better leave while he was still the helium hero. He walked around the Phantom, as if avoiding any contact with the thing, and said to Maggie, 'I'll see you later.'

Junior followed Ralphie out of the

68

barn. To make up for the fact that he had doubted Ralphie, he said, 'If you wait till Pap comes, you can pick up the helium in the truck.'

'No thanks,' Ralphie aid.

'It would be a lot easier.'

'Not really,' Ralphie said. Since he was going to have to steal the helium, the theft would be a lot less conspicuous by bike.

He pushed off and began the long ride home.

★　　★　　★

Michael and Vern were getting a drink of water at the sink.

'Well, I'll be going,' Michael said, wiping his mouth on the back of his hand.

'Don't forget to come back after supper,' Vern said. 'Because Junior insists we have to do it tonight.'

'I know. I will.' He paused, obviously reluctant to continue. 'Do you think your mom could call my mom?'

'What for?'

69

'To, you know, invite me?'

Vern had never heard of such an invitation, but he said, 'I'll ask.'

'Thanks.'

When Michael had gone, Vicki Blossom called, 'You kids come in the living room. I want to talk to you.'

Vern came in from the kitchen, Maggie from the porch. Vicki Blossom was sitting on the blanket-covered sofa, with one hand resting on the telephone.

She reached out both hands and put one on Maggie and one on Vern. She looked at them seriously. 'I want this night to be a success for Junior.'

'Mom, we do too,' Maggie said. Her mom was squeezing her and Vern together as if she were trying to make a tighter unit out of them. 'Mom, I want it more than anything,' Maggie said. This was the truth. Until Junior started feeling like a success again, she couldn't go back to her trick riding and enjoy her own success.

'It worries me that I can't be there to help, but I cannot leave the phone while Pap's missing.'

'We know that.'

70

'So you are taking my place. You two are Junior's mother for the night.'

Their mom was holding them together so tightly now that when they answered, they did it in unison. One person spoke instead of two. 'We will be.'

She hugged them. 'That's my kids.' She looked down at her watch, then at the phone. 'Where, where can Pap be? Vern, do you have any idea?'

Vern shook his head.

'Where do you usually go?'

'All over the county, Mom.'

Vicki Blossom sighed. 'Then I guess he could be anywhere.'

'Mom?' Vern asked.

'Don't bother me unless it's important.'

'It's important to me.'

'What?'

'Would you call Michael's mother and invite Michael to go with us tonight? His mom—'

'I will not tie up the phone with foolishness, and that is final. Now, go see if you can help Junior.'

RALPHIE'S THEFT

'Where are you going, Ralphie?'

Ralphie paused in the doorway with his bedroll under his arm. He looked surprised. 'I told you, Mom, I'm camping out at the Blossoms' farm tonight.'

'This is the first I've heard of any camp-out.'

'Mom, we've been planning it for a week.'

Ralphie was fairly sure he could get away with this lie. His mom had been upset all week. Another woman in town had started a rival balloon business, and the other woman was delivering her balloons while wearing a gorilla suit. Every time his mom saw a gorilla driving through town, with the back seat filled with balloons, it drove everything else out of her mind.

'Ralphie, you go over to the Blossoms too much. They're going to get tired of you.'

'His mom invited me. His mom has

excellent taste. She likes me.'

The phone rang at that moment, saving him. 'Oh, go on, go on,' she said.

'Thanks.'

Ralphie went into the garage, unrolled his mattress, and put the canister of helium inside. Fortunately this was his mother's spare canister. He would not have dared steal her only source of helium, because if she got an order and couldn't fill it and the gorilla lady could, she would never forgive him.

'What are you doing with Mom's helium?' a voice behind him asked. Ralphie turned, startled. It was Todd Lee, his youngest brother.

'Todd Lee, you've got eyes. What does it look like I'm doing?'

'Stealing Mom's helium.'

'This happens to be a defective can of helium, and it could explode at any minute. If it explodes while you are standing there making stupid remarks, you will end up splattered all over Mom's car, and you know how particular she is about the Blazer.'

73

'Mom!' Todd Lee yelled. He turned and flung open the door to the kitchen. 'Ralphie's stealing your—'

He didn't get to finish because his mother threw a dish towel at him. 'Will you kids stop bugging me for five minutes? You know who that was on the phone? That was an order for thirty-five message balloons, and after I had taken down the whole order, the man said, "Oh, by the way, you are the person who delivers in a gorilla suit, aren't you?" Now, get outside and stay there.'

Under his brother's suspicious gaze, Ralphie finished rolling his mattress around the helium and put it in the wagon. He secured the wagon behind his bike.

To his brother he said, 'If I were you, Todd Lee, I wouldn't even mention helium.'

Then he got on his bike and set out for the Blossoms' farm.

*   *   *

At seven-forty Ralphie pedalled up the

Blossoms' hill. He was feeling better. The initial shock of being caught stealing his mother's helium had worn off. If his brother told on him, as he probably would, and if his mother demanded an explanation, Ralphie would do something so unusual, so refreshing, his mother would be stunned. Ralphie would tell the truth.

'Mom, it was a situation where I could not refuse. Junior Blossom—he was the one that was in the hospital with me, remember? He was the one I almost ruined by taking him to the court-house when he had two broken legs. Well, furnishing the helium was my one chance to make up for that. I thought you would want me to.'

And then, 'The reason I didn't tell you was because you were upset by the gorilla woman and I did not want to add to your troubles.'

Anyway, if stealing helium was what it took to make Maggie smile at him, it would be worth it.

It was hard getting up the hill to the Blossoms with a can of helium behind his bike, but Ralphie tried not to let it show. Junior was the only one watching him, but Maggie might glance out of the window at any moment.

Junior was shading his eyes so he could see if what Ralphie was towing was helium. It was! Even though it was wrapped in a bedroll, Junior knew it was helium.

'Mom! Mom! He got it. The helium's here. Ralphie got the helium!'

'What'd you expect?' Ralphie stopped coolly beside the porch steps. 'Where do you want it, Junior?'

*   *   *

Inside the house, Vicki Blossom was dialing the phone. 'Hello, yes, officer, this is Vicki Blossom again. I called about a hour ago to ask if there had been any accidents reported in the county . . . Nothing? Well, I guess that's good, see, my father-in-law went off eight hours ago and he hasn't come back and I am just worried to death.'

Junior poked his head into the living room. 'He got it, Mom!'

His mom gave him an absent-minded

76

smile. Then she said into the phone, 'But my father-in-law is in his seventies, he is not in good health, and something is always happening to him. What I'm afraid of is that he's gone off the road in his truck and—'

She listened to the policeman.

'I know, well, officer, will you call me if you hear anything? It's not like him not to come home. It's not like him at all. You have my number?'

Junior had been waiting because his mom's absent-minded smile had not been enough recognition for the arrival of helium. She put the phone down with a worried look, so Junior thought she had not heard him the first time.

'It's here, Mom. The helium! The helium's here.' He flung his arms wide.

Every time Junior said the word *helium*, he imagined it floating upwards the way a bubble floats to the surface of water. He imagined the bubble popping somewhere in the stratosphere, and the word echoing throughout the universe. *Helium . . . helium . . . helium . . .*

'That's nice,' his mother said.

The phone rang, and she snatched it

from the receiver. 'Hello . . . Who? Michael?'

Vern heard the name and said quickly, 'That's probably for me, Mom.'

She ignored his outstretched hand.

'Michael, this is not the time for social calls. I am expecting a call from the police.'

There was a pause in which Vern again extended his hand for the phone.

'Well, I'm sorry you can't come without a personal invitation. Goodbye.'

'Mom!' It was a long cry of anguish from Vern.

His mother stopped it by drawing her finger across her throat. This was what their father always used to do to make them shut up, and it worked.

Vern turned. He walked stiffly out of the room, out of the house, across the yard, and kicked the first tree he came to.

★   ★   ★

Pap watched the sun go down from

inside the dumpster. It was a big red sun that hung over the purple ridges of mountains for a long time. Then it dropped with amazing speed behind the peaks and out of sight.

Pap felt a chill touch his bones.

'Boys,' he said, but he was speaking more to himself than to the dogs, 'I wonder if we'll still be here in the morning when the sun comes up.'

Then he sat down on the garbage bag to wait out the night.

UP, UP AND AWAY

'Now, you've got everything?'

'Yes.' Junior felt he had now answered that question at least a hundred times.

'You're sure?'

'Yes.'

'Maggie, does he have everything?'

'Yes, Mom, Ralphie checked.'

Vicki Blossom looked at the wagon where the Green Phantom was folded. The canister of helium was tied on top.

79

'I just wish I could go with you to make sure—'

'Mom, we'll be fine.'

'I wish you'd wait till tomorrow night, Junior.'

'Yeah, Junior,' Vern said quickly, 'because don't you want Michael to see it? Maybe Michael can come tomorrow night.'

Junior shook his head the way he did every time delay was mentioned. Vicki Blossom knelt beside him and put her hands on his shoulders. 'Junior, you do understand why I can't come, don't you?'

'Yes,' Junior said. He pulled away from her impatiently. The sun was setting. In half an hour it would be dark enough to launch.

His mother did not let him go. Junior sighed. 'You can't come,' he repeated, as if it were something he had learnt by heart, 'because Pap's missing and you need to wait by the phone.'

'Yes,' she said.

'But you're going to watch from the porch, and you know you'll get to see it. And if you do see it, you'll tell me all about it when I get home.'

Vicki Blossom smiled. 'Well, you better get going.'

That was what Junior had been trying to do. He picked up the handle of the wagon and began to pull it towards the woods. They had all agreed that the only place for the launch was Owl's Cliff, the highest point of land in the county. From Owl's Cliff the Green Phantom would float directly towards the city of Alderson.

Junior squared his shoulders for the journey. Owl's Cliff was a long way, and Junior was determined to pull the wagon by himself.

Vicki Blossom watched Junior and company disappear into the woods. She put her hands in her pockets and, shoulders sagging, sat down on the steps. She had a double feeling of doom—about her father-in-law and her son, and there was nothing she could do for either one of them. She wrapped her arms around her knees, as if for protection.

Junior pulled the wagon down the hill, through the chill waters of Snake

Creek, under the broken rail fence. When he started up Furnace Hill, he said graciously, 'Someone else can have a turn.'

* * *

It was cold in the dumpster. After the sun set, the warmth began to leave the metal sides, and Pap felt chilled. His lumber jacket was in the truck, but of course that didn't help him.

With the sun's warmth had gone the colour. There was still enough light to see by, but everything Pap saw was a dull grey. Pap felt increasingly tired, cold, and depressed. He wiped his face on his sleeve. He didn't even have the energy to pull out his handkerchief any more.

On his lap the puppy began to shiver. 'Get cold quick, don't it,' Pap said, 'and you know who the cold bothers most, don't you?'

The puppy curled himself into a tighter ball.

Pap sighed. 'It bothers the very young like you, and the very old like me.'

*   *   *

The Phantom had been unfolded, spread out on the grass, and filled with helium. Junior had even generously allowed Ralphie to help put in the helium. Well, maybe not generously. At first he had said to Ralphie, 'Get out of the way! Why is everybody getting in my way? Why is everybody trying to do everything? I will put in the helium all by myself!'

Ralphie had said, 'Fine,' and stepped back quickly. He held up both hands to show he was out of it. He folded his hands over his chest. 'Go right ahead and put in the helium all by yourself.'

It had taken Junior three minutes to realize that he did not know how to put in the helium. That was when he said generously, he thought, 'It's too dark. Somebody can help me with the helium.'

No one came forward, so Junior had glanced around as if deciding whom to bestow the favour on. 'Ralphie.'

83

Ralphie had pointed to himself and raised his eyebrows.

'Yes, you.'

Now that the helium was in the Phantom, Junior was determined to do the most important thing himself—the painting. 'Now don't help me even if I ask!' he said.

He took the paint can and began to shake it. The bead rattled inside. The shaking went on and on.

Finally, Ralphie said, 'If you'll allow me to make one suggestion, don't shake too long.'

Junior stopped. 'Why?'

'Well, it's your canister, of course, but I read in *Consumer Reports* that some cans were being recalled because little balls of dynamite had been accidentally put in the paint cans.'

'That's not true,' Junior said.

'Like I said, it's your can.'

Junior gave one final shake, a small one, and began to spray. He walked around the air mattresses, making wavy lines, filling them in. Around and around he went, pausing every now and then to give a small shake.

'Junior, if you're not careful, you're going to give out before you get to the garbage bags,' Maggie said.

Junior gave a trial shake. He realized the paint was almost gone. It was then that a blaze of inventiveness took over his mind, an unmistakable Junior touch—polka dots. He spaced the polka dots carefully around the garbage bags, and now he was through. The bottom of the Phantom was solid Day-Glo, a curved circle of eerie green, and the top was black with green polka dots. It took Junior's breath away.

'I'll carry it to the cliff myself.'

'Let it dry, Junior.'

Junior waited impatiently. He kept touching it until no green paint came off.

'Now really don't help me,' Junior said.

'Well, Junior, just let us help you get it over your head, all right? Just let us steady it.'

'All right, all right, all—'

Then the Phantom was above his head, and it was so awesome, Junior couldn't get out his last 'right'. Having the Green Phantom actually over him was the most wonderful experience of Junior's life. It was a huge, beautiful green blob that seemed to actually pull him skyward. Maybe helium did have a magnetic effect. Or maybe the Green Phantom actually wanted to take him along. Anyway, being pulled skywards by something as beautiful as the Phantom was a once-in-a-lifetime experience.

Junior felt lighter than air. He took a little springing step, and he and the Phantom bobbed upward. Junior leapt forward and it was one of the longest, lightest leaps of Junior's life.

Because the Phantom was so light and Junior's steps so long, Junior got to the edge of the cliff quicker than he would have liked. He wasn't prepared to let the beautiful green blob go yet.

He glanced over his shoulder. Maggie, Vern, and Ralphie were doing exactly what he wanted them to do—stand back in an admiring group. He got a wonderfully clear picture of the way he must look to them, standing here with the Green Phantom glowing over his head, giving him—

'What are you waiting for?' Ralphie asked in a voice that sounded, but couldn't possibly be, bored.

'A breeze, of course,' Junior answered.

The breeze seemed to be waiting just for Junior's words. Junior thought it was like a play they gave one time at school. A girl onstage said something about a breeze and instantly Jo-Jo Barwell had come floating on holding a sign that said BREEZE. Junior himself had been waiting to stamp on with a sign that said THUNDER.

Junior knew the breeze was coming because he heard it from far, far away. It started down at the bottom of the hill, where Snake Creek ran coldest, and it made leaves rustle the whole way up. Junior decided that when he felt the breeze on his back of his neck, he would let go. A breeze this perfect might only come along once a week, maybe once a month. He couldn't take a chance on missing it. Everything about this breeze told Junior this was the one.

He swallowed. A chill touched the back of his neck. Junior's heart moved up into his throat. He swallowed again. Then he opened his hands and let the Phantom go.

THE PHANTOM RETURNS

The Green Phantom pulled gently away from Junior's fingers and lifted with the breeze. Junior kept his hands in the air because if the Phantom came back, he wanted to be sure to catch it.

The Phantom was just beyond his grasp now. It was trembling in the air. To Junior it was like a creature struggling to draw its first breath. Then, before his gleaming eyes, the Phantom steadied and began floating away from the bluff.

It gave Junior a strange, scientific feeling. He knew the Phantom wasn't real. He knew it was only air mattresses and garbage bags and Day-Glo paint, and yet seeing something that strange and beautiful made him feel—well, maybe it wasn't a scientific feeling where everything happened according to law, this was more of a science fiction feeling where things happened the way you wanted them to happen.

The Phantom floated steadily away, a luminous, unearthly blob. And the polka dots—now Junior could hardly see the garbage bags, all he could see were the dots, floating over what looked like a flying saucer. The dots looked like satellites. Junior thanked his mind for giving him the idea of dots.

The Phantom rose higher. Now there were no garbage bags, no air mattresses. It was just a shape in the moonlight, a shape that man's eyes had never seen before. And over the shape hovered its satellites.

Abruptly the breeze shifted. Junior felt it, and his hands dropped to his cheeks. Maybe this had not been the perfect breeze after all, he thought with dismay. Maybe he had picked an imperfect breeze.

He gasped with real, physical pain. The Phantom was coming back, not going out over the world where Junior wanted it to go. It was coming back over Junior's head towards—Junior's hands covered his eyes. He couldn't look. The Green Phantom was going towards old man Benson's farm.

Junior was deathly afraid of old man Benson. He had been ever since he was four years old.

The day of his meeting with old man Benson had been the scariest day of Junior's life. It had started out to be a nice summer day. Junior had been passing old man Benson's farm, and he had noticed some tiny baby water-melons on some vines.

Junior had never seen baby water-melons before, and he had been so excited that he had ducked under the fence and walked into the garden. He went down the rows, admiring one baby water-melon after another, and then he had bent and touched one. He had not picked it or harmed it in any way—Junior would never have done such a thing. He just wanted to see if they were soft or hard.

As he touched, however, a long shadow fell over him. Junior glanced up. He was looking directly into the end of a double-barrelled shot-gun.

Junior gasped with fright. He fell back, sitting directly on two baby water-melons and crushing them.

Old man Benson said one word. 'Git.'

Junior said two. 'Yes, sir.'

Junior ran for home as fast as he could, and he had never laid eyes on old man Benson since. He never wanted to either.

'Maybe old man Benson will see it,' Ralphie said. Old man Benson was known countywide for his meanness. 'If he does, goodbye, Phantom.' Ralphie lifted a make-believe shot-gun. 'Pow! PowPowPow! Pow!'

Junior spun around, his face twisted with horror. He began to run towards old man Benson's farm. Ralphie's *pows* had gone straight to Junior's heart.

'Junior, wait,' Maggie yelled. Junior kept running. 'Come on, you guys,' Maggie said. 'We got to go with him.'

The three of them ran down the hill after Junior. 'Wait!' Ralphie said. Ralphie's voice had the sound of an army command, and even Junior paused. Ralphie pointed to show them that they were out-running the Phantom.

They looked skywards. The Phantom was directly over their heads, and it was beginning to sink. Junior raised his arms and coaxed it towards him with little pulling motions of his hands. The Phantom continued on course towards the Benson farm.

'I bet it's going to land in the garden,' Vern said.

That thought made tears come to Junior's eyes. He knew what old man Benson did to things that landed in his garden. 'I can't look,' he said. He covered his eyes. 'Tell me what happens.'

'Junior, open your eyes,' Maggie said. 'You're acting silly. The Phantom is not real. It's something you made. It's a thing.'

'It is not!'

'It is!'

'Not to me,' Junior said.

'Your sister's right,' Ralphie said. 'There are other air mattresses, other garbage bags, more'—he swallowed hard—'helium.' He hated to think he might have to use more of his mom's helium, but he had had enough running around the countryside for one night. His leg hurt and he wanted to be in his bedroll.

Junior's eyes were wide with astonishment. 'There's only one Green Phantom,' he said, 'can't you understand that? That is the only Green Phantom in the whole world!'

To Junior, this was true. Junior knew he could never do it again. He could never get the mattresses to bend the same way, never get those polka dots back in the exact same place. And even if he did, he wouldn't love the second Green Phantom as much as he loved this one.

The Green Phantom had now moved past the garden. It swept gently over the barn. It brushed the weather vane. The tip of the vane punctured one of the garbage bags, and this had a toppling effect. The Phantom began to go out of control.

Junior gasped with pain and fright.

Then everything happened at once. The helium went out of the garbage bag in a rush, and the Phantom began a downward spiral. There was a rustling sound, a gush of air, a moan. Every sound tore Junior's heart because these were the exact sounds, he knew, that a dying creature would make.

Then with one final, silken sigh, the Green Phantom came to its resting place—the roof of old man Benson's chicken house.

THE PHANTOM ON THE CHICKEN HOUSE

In silence the four of them took in this new development—the Green Phantom on the chicken house.

The only one of them who knew what to do about it was Ralphie, but he had decided not to be the one to say, 'Well, that's it, folks, one Green Phantom down the tube. Let's go home.' Ralphie knew that would be the signal for Junior to start crying again,

94

and while Junior would most likely end up in tears anyway, Ralphie did not want to be the one to cause them. Maggie had been giving him glances of admiration all day—first when he said he could get the helium, then when he got the helium, then when he put it in.

So Ralphie stood with his hands behind his back, waiting for someone else to break Junior's heart. He glanced sideways at Junior to see how he was taking it.

Junior was looking up at the chicken-house roof with his hands clasped beneath his chin. Probably praying, Ralphie thought.

Junior was praying, and he had been staring at the Phantom for so long that every now and then he thought his prayers had been answered. The Phantom actually seemed to slide off the chicken house, the way words slid off the page when he stared at them too long in school.

'It's coming,' he cried in one of those optimistic moments.

Dream on, Ralphie said silently.

'Well, maybe it's not coming right

now,' he said as his vision cleared, 'but I really think it's nearer the edge, don't you, Maggie?' Junior wisely asked the only person in the group who might spare him.

Maggie was taking her role as Junior's mother-for-a-night seriously, and she did exactly what she knew her mother would do. She put her arm around Junior's shoulder and squeezed him as hard as she could.

Junior knew the truth when he felt that arm on his shoulder. He waited, cringing, for the words that went with it.

'No, it isn't, hon. It's there to stay.'

If it had been his mother's real arm, that might have stopped Junior. But it was just his sister's. He squirmed out of Maggie's grasp, spun around and faced her. His hands were on his hips.

'It is not either there to stay!'

'Junior,' Maggie began. She reached out. Junior stepped back.

'It is not there to stay because I'm getting it down.' He jabbed his thumb against his chest.

'You can't get it down, Junior. You

know Mom doesn't allow you to get up on a chicken-house roof.'

'I'll do it,' Ralphie said wearily.

'You try to do everything!' Junior cried, turning on Ralphie. 'I'm getting sick and tired of you trying to take over. It's my Phantom, not yours, and I'm going to be the one to get it down!'

Ralphie gave another of his be-my-guest gestures, and Junior turned and set off for the chicken house. He did it so fast that there was a gasp of surprise from those he left behind.

Junior was halfway to the chicken house, out in the middle of the open yard, when he decided this might have been a good time to let Ralphie help if he really wanted to. Before he could do anything gracious, however, Ralphie and Vern rushed up, one on each side, and grabbed his arms. In a sort of lop-sided crouch—Ralphie's artificial leg held him back—they bore him to the chicken house.

Everything happened so fast then, Junior was helpless to change the outcome. Vern and Ralphie had their hands out, clasped together to boost him up. His foot went up into their hands. And then—this was so fast, it took Junior's breath, it was like Superman taking off from the earth—Junior was flung through the air. He landed flat on his stomach on the chicken-house roof.

He lay there, frozen with fear. At the same time the inside of his body—all the important things—seemed to have turned to jelly.

Junior's eyes were squeezed shut. He always shut his eyes when there was something he desperately did not want to hear. It never worked, but he couldn't stop himself from trying it. This time what Junior desperately did not want to hear was the sound of startled chickens.

Below him the hens were fluttering their wings and clucking to each other, responding to the soft thud they had heard, but it wasn't that shrill clucking that would wake old man Benson. After a long moment, Junior opened his eyes.

The Phantom was right there in front of him. He could reach out and touch it. This was a real relief to Junior. He wouldn't even have to stand up or anything—just give a little tug on the nearest air mattress. He tugged.

The Phantom bobbed towards him. One of the garbage bags brushed his forehead. Then the Phantom pulled back to its original place. Junior tugged again. Again the Phantom came so close, the garbage bag touched his head. Again it went back.

'It's stuck.' Junior breathed these words to himself. Slowly, carefully, he got to his feet. The roof had a steep slope, and Junior did not want to fall off. He glanced down to see if Vern and Ralphie were still there. They were, and so was Maggie. He felt a little better.

'Hurry!' Maggie hissed.

Junior put one finger to his lips in a plea for total silence. He took one step. He pulled again. He could see what the trouble was now. The wire between two of the air mattresses was hooked around the edge of the roof.

He would have to pull and lift at the same time. He got a good grip on the air mattress. His whole body was set to give the biggest pull of his life. He did this at the very moment when the Phantom released itself, just bounced up into the air.

The Phantom sailed up, over Junior's head, and onto the ground. Junior went down hard. The resulting bang as Junior struck the tin roof of the henhouse was like an explosion.

The chickens reacted immediately. There were instant shrieks of alarm and shrill cries. Within five seconds it seemed to Junior that a minimum of one thousand hens were flapping their wings and shrieking at the top of their lungs.

A dog began to bark at the house.

'The lights are on!' Vern yelled.

Ralphie saw a figure in the upstairs window. 'It's old man Benson,' he cried, 'and his shot-gun!'

The window was thrown up. The barrel of the shotgun came out. Maggie, Ralphie, and Vern bolted for the cornfield.

'We'll be back,' Maggie cried over her shoulder.

Junior watched them go, and the sight of them disappearing into the rows of corn was the worst thing he had ever seen in his life. Even Maggie's words brought him no comfort. He knew they would never come back. He never would have if he had gotten away.

Junior had always hated to be left behind, but there was something terrible and final about this particular desertion. In desperation, he looked down at the ground. It was a long way down. He could jump, but the last time he had done that, he had broken his legs.

Somebody tell me what to do, he begged.

It was old man Benson who made the decision for Junior. Old man Benson came out in the yard with his shot-gun.

Junior flattened himself against the roof. Old man Benson crossed the yard and looked at the Green Phantom. He walked around it. He kicked it with his foot. The Phantom responded with a light bounce.

Old man Benson walked around the

101

yard like a soldier on patrol. He looked behind the barn. He circled the henhouse. Junior did not breathe. Then old man Benson went to the house and sat down in a rocking chair on the porch. Junior knew the double-barrelled shot-gun was across his knees.

'Who was it?' his wife called.

'Some kids.'

'What were they after?'

'Some fool thing.'

'Come back to bed.'

'I'll set out here awhile. One of them said they'd be back.'

Junior let out all his breath in a long, hopeless sigh. He knew then that he would be spending the rest of his life on the roof of old man Benson's henhouse.

LEFT, ABANDONED, AND DESERTED

'Are you telling me that you left your own brother on the top of a chicken house?'

Vicki Blossom had been sitting on

the porch steps for over two hours, staring up at the night sky. She had wanted to see the Green Phantom so that she could truthfully tell Junior how beautiful it had been. At the same time she had been listening for the telephone.

As the hours passed, however, and the phone did not ring and she did not see the Phantom, her feeling of doom had increased. By the time she saw the kids running up the road, she knew the worst had happened.

She stood up. She made a quick head count. There were only three children running up the road. Junior was not one of them.

Vicki Blossom could not move for a moment. She just stood there waiting with a heart of lead for the bad news. Even so, it stunned her.

'You left Junior on the roof of a chicken house?' she asked again.

The living-room light was behind Vicki Blossom, so the children could not see her face, but none of them particularly wanted to. The way she was standing and the fury in her voice said it all.

Maggie was the oldest of the Blossom children, so she had felt it was her responsibility to break the news, to gasp out the original 'Mom, Junior's on the roof of old man Benson's chicken house.'

Vern said, 'We didn't do it on purpose, Mom.'

'Your own brother?'

Maggie hung her head in shame. This was the first time in weeks that her mother had been disappointed in her. Even when Maggie fell off Sandy Boy, her mother had praised her for trying with something like 'Almost!' Now Maggie was in disgrace and she knew it. What was worse, she deserved it. She had been Junior's mother for the night, and she had done the most terrible thing a mother could do—desert her child.

'And why, may I ask, did you let your brother climb up on a chicken house in the first place?'

'Mom, he wanted to,' Vern said.

'And you let him?'

'Mom—'

'Three big strong kids could not stop one little boy from climbing up on a chicken house? Is that what you expect me to believe?'

Maggie nodded dumbly.

'Not one of you had the guts to climb up on the chicken house yourselves?'

'We offered but—'

'I'm not interested in your offers, only your actions.'

They knew then that Vicki Blossom was not interested in their answers either. The three of them stood in silence.

'And then what? The three big strong kids ran off like cowards? I tell you one thing. If Junior hurts himself because of you, I will never forgive any of you. Never!'

Ralphie cleared his throat. 'What Maggie didn't tell you, Mrs Blossom, was that Mr Benson had a gun. It was pointed right at us. If we hadn't left when we did, one or more of us might be dead.'

'You don't die of rock salt wounds,' Vicki Blossom said, but she didn't look at Ralphie. She wasn't through with

Maggie and Vern. She stood there, glaring at them, piercing the darkness with her glances. They were the ones she was furious with. Oh, she was furious with Ralphie too, but Blossoms knew better than to run off and leave another Blossom.

Ralphie spoke again. He knew Mrs Blossom had no interest in him, but he couldn't help himself. He could see from the way Maggie's shoulders were drawn up that she was getting ready to cry, and he did not want to see Maggie cry. He had seen her brush tears from her eyes with the tips of her braids and that had been bad enough, but if she cried . . .

'Mrs Blossom, I'll be glad to go back after him,' Ralphie said quickly, 'I—'

'I'm going after him myself, thank you very much.'

Vicki Blossom came down the steps loudly. It was as if she had on combat boots instead of sneakers. There was a small space between Vern and Maggie, and she went right through it, pushing them to either side.

She strode past Ralphie without a

glance and then strode—there was no other word for the way she was walking—down the road.

The children were so stunned by her fury that they were a little late starting after her. That was exactly what Vicki Blossom had been hoping they would do—start after her. She spun around.

She was in the shadows of the pine trees, so it was still impossible to see her eyes, but Ralphie had seen his own mom's eyes under similar conditions, and he knew what they looked like.

'Oh no you don't!'

The children stopped in their tracks.

'Oh no you don't!'

She managed to put new meaning into the words this time, making it even more of a command. 'You stay right where you are, every living, breathing one of you.'

That took in them all. No one moved a muscle.

'You left Junior. You deserted Junior. You abandoned Junior. And as far as I am concerned you aren't worthy to help Junior. Junior doesn't want your help.'

All of them knew this was a lie, but no one dared speak.

'What do you want us to do?' Maggie asked finally. Ralphie hated to hear her voice tremble like that.

'Can't you even figure that out? Can't you do one single thing for yourselves? No, I guess you can't. You proved that tonight. I gave you a chance to do one simple thing for me, and you proved you cannot do anything, especially when courage and loyalty are called for.'

She drew in a long breath. 'All right. Here it is. Maggie, you and Vern go in the house and sit by the phone and wait for Pap's call. No courage will be called for. No loyalty. Just sit by the phone and answer it if it rings. Do you think you can do that? Do you think you can manage to do that one simple thing without messing up?'

'Yes.'

'And you'—she pointed at Ralphie— 'you go home.'

'Yes, ma'am,' Ralphie said.

Vicki Blossom turned and began striding down the road again. There was a pause, and then Ralphie manfully took command of the group. 'We better,' he said, 'do exactly what she said.'

Maggie hesitated a moment. She was holding her braids against her cheeks, so she would be ready for the tears when they came. Then she called, 'Mom, please be careful. He really does have a gun.'

Without turning around, Vicki Blossom answered, 'I can handle Benson.'

'I'm sorry!' Maggie called.

This time there was no answer. Maggie turned—she needed her braids now—and ran into the house.

JUNIOR AND *THEM*

Junior had not moved a single muscle except his throat muscle in fifteen minutes. He would not have moved that except that he was desperately afraid he was going to cough, and the only way for him to keep from coughing was to swallow. His swallows sounded, to him, as loud as gulps.

Fifteen minutes more passed slowly by. Junior had now been stranded on top of the chicken house for a long thirty minutes. Old man Benson had been sitting on the front porch with his double-barrelled shot-gun, waiting, for the same length of time.

In those thirty minutes, Junior had come to realize that the roof of a chicken house was a terrible place to be. It was such a terrible place that parents could even threaten their kids with it. 'You behave yourself or I'm putting you up on top of a chicken house!'

Finally, finally, Junior heard old man Benson get up. He heard the rocking chair keep on rocking a little. He heard old man Benson walk to the edge of the porch. Then he heard old man Benson walk across the porch, open the door, go inside, and close the door behind him.

Junior had spent most of the thirty minutes on the chicken house praying for this to happen. 'Please let him go in the house, please please let him go in the house, please please, please let him go in the house.' He had added so many *pleases*, he had lost count.

So he felt a great moment of relief when his prayers were finally answered. He waited until the bedroom light went out, and then he allowed himself the quiet, muted cough that had been in his throat so long. As it turned out, it was not just one cough, it was a series of coughs.

Junior clapped his hand quickly over his mouth. The coughs kept coming.

Immediately he heard a ruffling of feathers beneath him. There were a couple of startled cackles, then the beating of wings, some miscellaneous *bruck-bruck-bruckkkkks*. He had come to particularly dread those *brucks*.

He swallowed his remaining coughs, and the chickens grew quieter. This did not give Junior a lot of comfort, however, because he now understood the situation. Old man Benson thinks we've all gone home, but THEY—that was how he thought of the chickens—THEY know better. They

111

know one of us is still here, and they know it's me.

'Please let them think I've gone,' he began to pray. 'Please please let them think I've gone. Please please please—'

Junior broke off. His body hurt too much to go through all the *pleases* again. Even though the *pleases* had finally worked, he hurt too much.

Junior was lying on his stomach, and since the roof had a steep slope, Junior's head was pointing towards the ground.

His hip-bones hurt, his knees hurt, his ribs hurt. His toes really hurt. His toes were hooked over the peak of the roof to keep him from sliding down the slope. When Junior got off the roof, if he ever did, his toes would probably be frozen in this position, for days, weeks even, maybe for the rest of his life.

Tears kept filling his eyes, but because he was upside down, they couldn't roll down his cheeks like tears were supposed to do. They dropped off his face between his eyebrows.

Junior's left ear hurt too. It was pressed against the roof, and in the thirty minutes that he had spent on the roof, Junior had learnt a lot about chickens through that ear.

It seemed to him that there were three hens who were causing all the trouble, and these three hens were making it impossible for any of the other chickens to sleep. And if the chickens didn't sleep, Junior couldn't move, and if Junior couldn't move, Junior couldn't get down, and if Junior couldn't get down—

Junior broke off. It was exactly like a story Junior's teacher had read them last year. Junior could hear his teacher saying the last, sad line of the story, 'And Junior will not get home tonight.'

Junior's mind kept going after his teacher's sentence stopped. 'And if Junior doesn't get home tonight, Junior will still be up here in the morning when old man Benson comes out to feed the chickens.'

Junior shuddered slightly at the thought, and the three leaders of the chickens reacted with fluttering wings, more cries of *bruck-bruck-bruckkkk*. Oh, be quiet, Junior said, go to sleep. Lay some eggs. Haven't you got anything better to do than squawk?

Maybe, Junior thought suddenly, I should just go for it. Maybe I should unhook my toes, pull my legs around and jump off the roof.

That was exactly what he would have done a year ago. But one of the last things the doctor had told Junior was no more jumping off high places. 'You land hard on those legs again, and you'll most likely be right back in hospital.' Junior would almost rather be up on top of a chicken house than in the hospital.

And maybe, his dismal thoughts continued, if he let go with his toes, he might slide off the roof before he had a chance to turn himself around. He had a clear picture of himself, arms extended, plunging into the hard earth. Breaking both your arms couldn't be much better than breaking both your legs.

Maybe, he thought, and another tear rolled off his eyebrow, maybe I should just do the sensible thing and stay up here for the rest of my life.

THE NIGHTMARE

Pap was asleep, and Pap was having a nightmare. In his nightmare he was trapped in a garbage dumpster, only the garbage dumpster of his dream was filled with liquid garbage and Pap was drowning in it.

First the garbage had been up to his chest, then his chin, and now it was over his head. The garbage was like quicksand. It kept pulling him under. It was all Pap could do to come up for air.

Pap went down once, twice. He struggled up for one last breath. Then he was going down into the garbage for the last time.

At that moment Pap was awakened by being hit on the head with a bag of garbage. 'What—what?' he cried. He batted at the air.

The plastic bag broke. Garbage rained around him. He reacted by trying to do what he had been trying to do in his nightmare—get his head above garbage.

His arms were swimming frantically though the loose garbage, but as in his nightmare, he couldn't get high enough. He tried to push to the surface with his legs, but they were useless.

In a desperate move, Pap braced his hands on his knees. He forced himself to his feet.

Then Pap heard a woman scream.

That scream brought Pap back into the real world. He was in a dumpster, but it wasn't full of liquid garbage, just everyday real garbage. So the scream had to be real too. That meant someone was here! Someone was outside! Someone had thrown garbage on him!

'Wait! Help! Help! Help!'

Pap peered over the side of the dumpster. A woman was backing away in open-mouthed horror. When she saw his face, she screamed again and broke into a run for her car. He caught a glimpse of her terrified face as she ran through the car's headlights.

'Please help me, please! I ain't gonna hurt you. I can't hurt nobody.'

The woman got into the car. She

slammed the door and locked it. Then she peered at Pap through the windshield. She looked as if she'd seen a ghost.

Pap realized then how unkempt he must appear. He attempted to smooth his hair. Then he extended both his arms. 'Please, lady, oh, please. Do the Christian thing.' He smoothed his hair again. 'Help an old man. I'm dying, lady. I tell you I'm dying!'

The woman started the car.

Tears rolled down Pap's cheeks. 'Please, lady, please! I meant it when I said I'm dying. I can't stand to be in this dumpster no more. Help me, lady, help me.'

He had one last glimpse of the woman's horrified expression as she turned the steering wheel. She drove out of the parking lot so fast that the tyres spun in the loose sand.

'I can't hurt nobody,' Pap called after her. He stretched out one hand. 'I'm helpless.'

Pap watched until the tail-lights were specks in the distance. He kept standing there. He was so tired and worn down that he suspected he had told the truth when he had said he was dying.

'Well, there went another one,' Pap told Mud. He made an effort not to let his despair show in his voice. Mud was sensitive to sounds.

Then he sat down and told Dump the same thing in a lower, sadder voice. 'There went another one.' Dump pawed Pap's leg, asking to get back in Pap's lap.

Pap picked him up without even knowing he did so. In his mind was the thought that had begun when the woman drove away. It would be a terrible, terrible thing for a man to die in a dumpster.

JUNIOR'S MOVE

Junior had decided to make his move. The chickens had not clucked loudly in at least five minutes, and Junior knew it was time. He had to do something, because it seemed to him the sky was beginning to get light in the east. The last thing in the world Junior wanted to hear was the crow of a rooster. Then it would all be over but the words 'Climb down with your hands over your head.'

At last Junior had a plan. The plan came about because Junior remembered a wonderful thing. There had been a window on the side of the chicken house. He had seen it briefly on that incredibly fast boost up, but it was a window and Junior thought there was a little window ledge.

Junior's plan was to swing down, feel for the ledge with his feet, put his feet firmly on the window ledge, and step down to the ground. The plan was foolproof if, he added, the ledge was there.

Junior knew there was a possibility it was not. Sometimes his eyes saw things that Junior wanted them to see. Like last Christmas, Junior had tiptoed down the steps in the middle of the night and his eyes had seen a red bicycle under the tree with his name on it. When he came down the next morning, the bicycle was not there.

Junior began moving snakelike towards the side of the chicken house. He began to breathe easier. He was going to make it. He knew he was. He would be home in his bed before morning.

In that moment of relief Junior realized that the lights had gone on once again in the Bensons' bedroom. He glanced up, horrified. He had been so intent on his own silent, stealthy movements that he had forgotten about the house. He had been worrying about THEM, the chickens, when what he should have been worrying about was HIM. Was he coming back out? Had he seen Junior? Would he have his shot-gun?

The porch lights went on. Old man Benson *was* coming back out. He would spot Junior for sure this time. He might even shoot before—

At that moment he heard something he had never expected to hear again in this world. He heard his mother's voice. Then he realized that his mother was knocking at the door. 'Open this door, Mr Benson,' she was saying. 'I mean to talk to you.'

Junior heard the door open.

His head was raised high now because he did not want to miss one single word of his mother's wonderful voice. She had the most wonderful voice of anyone in the world, and her words were always perfect. These were more than perfect.

'Mr Benson, I believe my son is on the roof of your chicken house, and I have come to take him home.'

Junior leaned over the roof and peered down. The window was there, just as he remembered, and it did have a ledge. His eyes had been right this time. Junior slung one leg over the side of the roof and got ready to swing down.

'And what's more,' his mother said. Junior stopped. What more could there be? Hadn't she just said it all with her forceful voice? 'I believe my son is on the roof of your chicken house, and I have come to take him home?'

Not quite, Junior discovered.

'And that thing over there is the Green Phantom, and I am coming back for that in the morning.'

Junior swung himself off the chicken house. His feet felt for, and found, the ledge. Junior stepped down.

He patted the chicken house. 'Good night ladies,' he told the hens, and then he ran across the moonlit yard and into his mother's arms.

*　　　*　　　*

Ralphie was in his bedroll, his artificial leg at his side, and he was very glad to be there. He had done all the running and bike riding that he could take. His leg hurt badly.

He looked up at the stars. He had spread out his bedroll in the pine trees, hidden from Mrs Blossom—who had told him in no uncertain terms to go home—and yet where he could see the stars. Gradually, the stars and the soothing sound of the crickets and tree frogs were making him forget his leg and a trying day.

Just then he heard voices. He flipped over onto his stomach and lifted a pine branch. It was Mrs Blossom and Junior returning from the Benson farm.

Ralphie let the branch down so it hid his pale face. As they passed, Junior waved his arms triumphantly in the air. 'Mom, the Phantom was sooooo beautiful. I just can't describe it. It was absolutely, positively the most beautiful thing in the whole world.'

Ralphie shook his head, lowered it, and fell asleep.

BLESS YOU; OFFICER

A police car pulled into the dumpster parking lot at one o'clock in the morning. The blue light was flashing, but Pap didn't see it. Pap was asleep, and this time it was a deep, dreamless sleep. Pap was snoring.

He awakened with a snort when both policemen shone flashlights directly into his face. His eyes opened. He was instantly blinded, and he put one trembling hand up to protect himself.

He heard the words, 'What are you doing in the dumpster, sir?'

Pap couldn't see the men, but from the official tone of the question, he knew they were policemen. Relief rushed through his aching body with such speed, it brought tears to his eyes.

He had a desperate struggle getting to his feet, especially with Dump in one hand. 'Bless you, bless you for coming,' he said. He reached out to them with his free hand. 'I fell in and couldn't get out. Don't leave me. Oh, please don't leave me.'

'Here,' the policeman said. 'Let me help you, sir.' Pap felt one policeman take his hand, and the other took his elbow. They steadied him.

'Oh, I thank you.'

When he was on his feet at last, he put the hand holding Dump over his heart to show how grateful he was. 'Bless you. And if you'll just hand me that little ladder that's lying over there, I'll be getting out of here.'

The policeman got the ladder, folded it, and handed it up to Pap.

'Thank you. Bless you,' Pap said.

'If you tell me where your keys are,' the other policeman said, 'I'll back your truck over and you can step out onto the back.'

'Oh, bless you.' Pap had already started thinking with dread of that terrible moment when he would have to balance on the side of the dumpster, reach down, pull the ladder up, and then climb down. Even with the policemen there to break his fall, it would be dangerous. 'The keys are in the ignition.'

The policeman went to the truck. When Pap heard the familiar rattle of the truck's engine, he thought he was going to weep.

He took the ladder in a hand that still trembled. 'Can I trouble you to take my dog.' He passed Dump out to the policeman. 'He's how I come to get in this mess in the first place. Somebody left a dog in the dumpster, and I was going to help him out, ended up falling in myself.'

The policeman put Dump down on the ground. Mud had been watching for this with his good eye, and he did what he had been waiting ten hours to do. Mud smelt him. The puppy had

125

enough sense to lie down and let himself be smelt.

Inside the dumpster, Pap brushed some garbage aside with his boot, and settled the ladder in a steady position. He began to climb out. Both policemen extended their arms and gripped him tightly as he went over the top.

'I didn't think I was ever—thank you both so much—going to be found. Thank you,' he said again as they supported him. He leaned back to get the ladder, but the policeman said, 'We'll do that for you, sir, you just step on over onto your truck.'

'Thank you. I didn't think I was—bless you—going to last the night. Thank you.'

Now he was on the back of his own truck, but he was so unsteady, he had to lean over and clutch the sides. 'I'm all right,' he told the policemen. They were putting the ladder by the truck so he could climb down. 'How did you ever come by the dumpster? How did you find me? Thank you. Did you hear my dog howling or what?'

'Some woman called us. You scared

her to death. She threw in some garbage and you came up yelling at her.' The policeman laughed. 'The woman said, "There's a crazy man in a dumpster on the Stone Church Road".'

'Oh, bless her heart. What a kind woman.' Pap snapped his ladder shut and shoved it in the back of the truck. He picked up the puppy.

Mud wasn't through smelling the puppy, and he followed Pap to the door of the truck, with his nose in the air.

Pap put the puppy on the front seat. 'Get in back, Mud,' he said. He turned once again to the policemen.

'Sirs, I thank you once again for your help and I bless you with all my heart.'

'You take care, sir. You find any more dogs in dumpsters, you give us a call.'

'I will. I will.'

'If you don't mind my saying so, a man your age shouldn't be—'

'I know. I know.'

Mud was already in the back of the truck. He wanted to go home as much as Pap. When he got home, the first thing he planned to do was finish smelling the puppy.

Pap was still trembling. He paused to grip the door for support. The policeman started forward, but Pap waved him away.

'I'm all right. I just need to go home and get in my bed.' And then Pap climbed in the truck and drove away.

THE BACK HALF
OF THE DOG

Vicki Blossom lifted her head. She heard the rattle of Pap's truck as it drove over the bridge, the backfire as it started up the hill. She got up and ran out on the porch.

She could see the reflection of the dim headlights, and she put one hand over her heart in relief. It was two o'clock in the morning, and Vicki Blossom had not been to bed. She had been by the telephone all night, wrapped in a blanket, waiting for some news.

'Pap!' she cried. She rushed down

the steps, the blanket flaring behind her like a cape, and waited by the grease-stained weeds where Pap always parked. When the truck stopped, she said, 'Pap, where on earth have you—'

She broke off. She was struck by how tired Pap looked, how deep the lines in his face were. For the first time she thought of him as an old man.

She leaned in the cab and put one hand on his wrist. In a gentler voice she said, 'Pap, are you all right?'

'I'm as all right as I can expect to be,' he said.

He turned off the ignition. The truck shuddered, the motor died, but Pap continued to sit there, staring at the dashboard. His whole body sagged with age and fatigue.

'What does that mean—as you can expect to be?' When he didn't answer, she squeezed his wrist, 'Pap, talk to me. I've been frantic!'

For the first time, Pap was aware of her hand on his wrist. He twisted free. 'Don't touch me. I'm too nasty to touch.'

'What happened?'

'Oh, it's a long, sad story about an old clumsy man and a dumpster.'

He reached down and picked up Dump with one hand. Mud was already out of the truck, waiting by the door, wagging his tail in anticipation. Both eyes were open now.

'Something happened at the dumpster?' Vicki prompted him.

'I don't want to tell you.'

'Pap, this is Vicki. You can tell me anything.'

'I'd hate for this to get around.'

'I won't tell a soul, Pap, I won't even tell the kids if you don't want me to.'

'It's the kind of thing that could, well, make a man look foolish.'

'Pap, you could never look foolish to me. You are the best friend I have in the world.'

'Well . . .'

He climbed out of the truck and put the puppy down. Mud rolled Dump over and began to smell him.

'Pap, tell me! Talk to me! Pap, I have been frantic. I have called the hospital. I have called the police. I have called everybody I know in this county.

What happened to you?'

Pap took a deep breath. He wondered if he would ever get over smelling like garbage. With what dignity he could, he said, 'I spent the night in a dumpster.' He started limping towards the house.

Vicky stepped over the puppy. She took the blanket from her shoulders and wrapped it around Pap's. She followed him to the porch with one hand on his back. 'How did you get in the dumpster?'

'Fell.'

'How did you get out?'

'Police.'

'How?'

'I would take it as a very kind favour, Vicki,'—he paused without looking at her—'if that could be the end of our talk about the dumpster.'

'Well, of course it's the end of the talk. I'll never mention it again, only what, may I ask, are you doing bringing another dog home?'

'I knowed that was coming.'

'Well, we don't need another mouth to feed. We—'

'The dog's name is Dump and I brought him home as a present for the boys.'

'The boys have a dog—Mud.'

They started up the steps. Pap was holding on to the rail with one hand, his blanket with the other. He went up a step at a time, like a child. As he paused on the third step, he said, 'No, Mud is my dog, always has been, always will be. Over yonder is the boys' dog—Dump.' He yelled, 'Mud, let that puppy go. That puppy don't need you holding him down to the ground. Let him up now.' Then he limped tiredly into the house.

★   ★   ★

Junior and Vern found out at the breakfast table that they were the owners of a dog named Dump. It caught them by surprise because both of them had their minds on other matters. Junior was thinking of going with his mom back to old man Benson's to get the Green Phantom, and he was planning how old man Benson would look when he saw Junior walking boldly in beside his mother. Vern was wondering how to ask his mom to call Michael's mother and invite Michael to the second launch.

'A dog?' they said together.

'Yes.'

'Why are we getting a dog?' Vern asked. 'I thought Mud was our dog.'

'Mud's my dog. Dump is yours, and I want you to share this dog now.'

'We will,' Junior said happily. Junior loved to share. He had never been able to understand people who didn't.

'The dog is half yours and half yours.'

Again Junior nodded. He was just getting ready to ask where the dog was when Vern said quickly, 'I claim the front half.' Vern was terribly pleased. He would never have thought of staking the claim if Michael had not told him that he had done this one time to his sister over their horse Daisy. He flushed with pleasure.

Junior was so surprised that he said the first thing that popped into his mind. 'I claim the back half.'

He put his hands over his lips. Then he opened them like double doors. 'I meant to say that I claim the front half too.'

'Boys,' Pap said. 'Now go on outside and see your dog. He's spent most of the night being pestered by Mud and he would probably like to do something else for a change.'

Junior got up so fast, his chair tipped over. He went out the door calling, 'Dump, here, Dump.' Over his shoulder he said to Vern, 'I'll share my half with you if you'll share yours with me.'

'Oh, all right,' Vern said. He had had the pleasure of staking the claim. Now he wanted to see what he'd claimed. They ran out onto the porch together.

*   *   *

'Maggie?' Vicki Blossom came into Maggie's room. 'Are you still sleeping?'

'No, I just didn't feel like getting up.'

Vicki sat down on Maggie's bed. She twisted one of Maggie's braids around her finger. 'Are you upset about what I said last night?'

Maggie shook her head.

'You're sure?'

'Everything you said was true.'

'No, it wasn't. I was upset. I was worried about Pap. I was worried about Junior. And I'm just not one of these people who go around acting calm when I'm worried and upset.'

'I don't expect you to be.'

'Will you forgive me?'

'Will you forgive me?'

'I sure will,' Vicki Blossom said. 'Now, get up. We've got to get the Greeeeen Phantom!'

★   ★   ★

'Mom?'

'What, Vern?'

Vern had waited to ask the question until they were almost home with the Green Phantom. 'Can I ask you a favour?'

'Oh, I guess so, only, remember, I'm busy this afternoon. I've got to work until five.'

'I know. This won't take but a minute. Will you call Michael's mom and invite him to go to the launch with us tonight?'

'Oh, I guess so, Vern. But I don't see why he can't just come.'

'Because, Mom, everybody's family is not like ours.'

THE GREEN PHANTOM PARTY

Every single person in the world that Junior loved was coming to the second launching of the Green Phantom, Vern, Pap, Mom, Mud, his own dog Dump, Michael, Ralphie, and Maggie. Junior went over the guest list again and again. Each time he saved the best name for last. Mad Mary.

'Is she really and truly coming?' he had asked Pap. Pap was the one who had delivered the invitation to Mad Mary.

'She says she is, but you know Mary. Sometimes she'll do what she says and sometimes she won't.'

Junior knew Mad Mary better than that. 'If she says she'll come,' he had said, nodding emphatically, 'she'll come. Tell me about it one more time.'

'I told you twice.'

'Once more. Please.'

'Well, I passed her on the road this morning. She was picking up a nice squirrel that had been lightly tapped by a pick-up truck. She straightened up and waved, and so I stopped. The woman is getting downright sociable. Anyway, she came over to the truck to show me the squirrel and she said, "What's Junior up to? I don't see Junior much these days."'

Junior stood there beaming. He loved to hear things people said about him. 'Go on,' he prompted.

'Mary said, "You'd think since I pulled him out of the coyote trap, he'd be grateful and come see me more. He hasn't been in any trouble, has he?"'

'I says, "Would you call getting stuck on top of old man Benson's chicken coop trouble?" She says, "Oh, oh, oh," because old man Benson fired his shot-gun at her one time; the rock

137

salt actually left holes in her hat. The man aimed at her head! Get her to show you them holes sometime. Well, then I told her about your UFO and she told me—'

'No, tell it like it happened, the exact words—what you said and she said.'

'Well, I said, "Junior made a UFO, and he's going to send it up again tonight. He'd be proud to have you come."'

'No, you skipped some of it. She said, "What was he doing up on old man Benson's chicken house?" That's the part you skipped. That's one of my favourite—'

'Junior, you know this better than I do. I can't stand here putting on a production for you. I got chores. I told you twice and that's enough. She'll come if she comes, and that is that.'

Even though Junior knew Mad Mary would be there, he ran ahead of everybody so he would be the first one to see her. He crossed his fingers as he came over the crest of Owl's Hill.

'She's here,' he shouted down the hill. 'I told you she'd come.'

Mad Mary was sitting on a rock with her ragged skirts all spread out around her and her cane braced against the ground. It was the way queens sat, Junior thought, in olden times. He ran over and put his head on her lap, the way subjects used to do, also in olden times. He breathed in the dusty, outdoorsy smell of her skirts.

Mad Mary patted him on the head with her gnarled fingers. 'I haven't seen you in weeks. I thought you were going to come see me.'

'I am! I've got to launch my Green Phantom before I can do anything,' Junior cried happily. He loved having too much to do. 'Then I'll come.'

'Where is this Phantom that's been getting you in so much trouble?'

'In the wagon. Here it comes now.'

'I hear it landed you on top of a chicken house.'

'Old man Benson's,' Junior said proudly.

Vern and Michael came into view first, pulling the wagon, then Pap and Vicki Blossom followed, then Maggie and Ralphie. It was exactly like a procession, Junior thought.

'And I've got a new dog!' Junior turned his glowing face back to Mary. 'You'll get to see him. He's coming. Mud is a little bit jealous of him and he puts his foot on Dump when nobody's looking and holds him down—that's probably where Dump is now, being held down. Pap, will you please call Mud? I want Mary to see Dump.'

Pap whistled, and in a few minutes Mud came leaping over the brush. A few minutes later Dump ran into the clearing too.

Michael was standing back from the group, partly because he was awed by Mad Mary, partly because he was awed by the occasion. This was the most exciting night of Michael's life, and it followed the most miserable, a night when he had lain awake, his face turned to the window, trying for a glimpse of the Phantom.

He had thought he had missed it, and then that morning had come the phone call, the invitation. He had had to listen to a fifteen-minute lecture from his mother about behaving himself, but it was worth it. He was here with the Blossoms.

Vern came back and said, 'Come on, Michael.'

'I am.'

'Mad Mary won't hurt you.'

'I know.'

Vern stood for a moment, sensing that Michael was awed by his family. All this time he had been envying Michael's family, and now Michael envied his. Vern didn't understand exactly why this was true, but it made him feel better, more secure in his friendship.

'Everybody's here,' Junior cried. Michael and Vern joined the circle. Now Junior was surrounded by every single person in the world that he loved, and this caused him to spin around with pleasure. His arms were out like aeroplane wings. He was so happy, he felt he could take off and fly himself.

His spin came to a stop, and he looked around. 'Is everybody ready?'

'Whenever you are,' his mother said.

'All right. I'll start setting things up,'

Junior said. He crossed to the wheelbarrow, brushing his hands on his T-shirt.

THE LAUNCH

'Doesn't it look beautiful?' Junior asked.

The Phantom was now laid out on the ground. The three air mattresses were in a circle, the garbage bags were crumpled up in the centre. The polka dots glowed dully in the creases.

Junior stood there, admiring it. He could feel that everyone else was doing the same thing, because they were standing so still. It was as if they couldn't believe the Phantom was real.

The only person who had spoken was Mad Mary, and all she had said was, 'My, my.' Junior took those two 'My's as a very high compliment indeed.

'Ralphie, you can help me put in the helium,' Junior said. Even Ralphie was behaving right this time, waiting to be asked.

'My pleasure,' Ralphie said.

Ralphie came forward. In the middle of last night, as Ralphie lay awake in his sleeping bag, he had made a vow never to steal his mother's helium again, not even for Maggie. It was too risky, especially when someone as unstable as Junior was concerned. After that vow, he made another. He would do everything he possibly could to make this second flight of the Phantom an absolute total success. Then there would never have to be a third.

Also, Ralphie had admitted to himself that there had been something about the way the Phantom sort of swam through the air that had surprised him. He wouldn't go as far as to say the Phantom had been beautiful, but it certainly had not been ugly. On a scale of one to ten, the flight had been a good solid seven.

Ralphie allowed Junior to think he was doing it, but Ralphie got the helium in exactly the way he wanted it and taped the bags shut exactly the way he wanted that done. Then he said, 'Good job, Junior!'

Ralphie and Junior stood up together. Ralphie moved over beside Maggie. Maggie had been holding the Phantom down in case the wind came up.

Junior walked slowly around the Phantom, admiring it, checking it. When he saw that it was perfect, he wiped his hands once again on his shirt.

'I'm ready,' he said.

Maggie and Ralphie lifted the Phantom, and Junior moved under it. For a moment he couldn't breathe.

The Phantom was so big and so beautiful that it just seemed to pull Junior up to the sky. He looked up into the depths of the garbage bags. He wanted to explain to the Phantom that he would go along if he could, but somehow it seemed to him that the Phantom understood.

Junior started for the cliff. He had already decided he was not going to make any of the same mistakes he had made last time, mistakes like walking too fast and getting to the edge of the cliff before he was ready to let the Phantom go.

This time he went to the cliff like a bride, closing each step. He stood there with the Phantom over his head, his eyes on the lights of Alderson. His heart was beating so hard, he wondered if he would be able to hear the breeze.

As if on cue, it started. Junior heard the faint rustling of leaves down behind the hill. The breeze was on its way. Goose bumps rose on Junior's arms.

Then the wind was there, and it seemed to just sweep the Phantom from Junior's hands. It was breathtaking the way the wind managed the whole thing. It was as if this particular wind had been created specifically to carry his Phantom up into the heavens.

Junior remained with his arms lifted, his mouth open, his heart pounding, and he watched his Phantom rise towards the star-filled sky.

Everyone was looking up at the sky, so Mud put his paw on Dump and pushed him to the ground. Mud knew he was not supposed to do this—Pap had been telling him not to all day, but Mud couldn't help himself.

Every time he saw the puppy

running around like he was having a good time, Mud had to put his paw on him. He had to.

This time the puppy had been chasing a cricket, running after it when it jumped, poking his nose down into the grass. Then the cricket would jump again and the puppy would run after it.

When Mud had the puppy pinned securely on the ground, he glanced up at Pap to see if Pap had noticed. No, Pap was looking at the sky like everyone else. For once Mud could pester the puppy in peace.

THE LAST CHANCE

The Phantom was making those slow, underwater motions that were so especially beautiful to Junior. Every time the Phantom swam like that, Junior would swear on a Bible it was alive. It had to be. Nothing that wasn't real could move in that naturally graceful way.

Junior felt he could stand here for the

rest of his life, staring up at the sky, watching the Phantom. The Phantom was, Junior thought, his own personal design and yet somehow it no longer belonged just to him. Somehow it now belonged to the—

He never got to finish the beautiful thought that the Phantom now belonged to the world, because behind him someone gasped.

Then he distinctly heard his mom murmur, 'Oh, no.'

'What? What?' Junior cried.

At first he had merely been sort of irritated at the gasp because it broke what was, to him, a religious silence. Now he felt genuine alarm.

'Maybe it's nothing, hon,' his mom said, 'I don't really know anything about it, but—'

She didn't have to finish. Junior saw it too, and it was definitely not 'nothing'. The Phantom had stopped turning. It was motionless in the air. Something was wrong.

'It's exactly like last time,' Junior said. 'Only last time—' Junior didn't get to finish. Because, exactly like last

147

time, the Phantom began turning in the opposite direction. Once again, the wind had shifted.

'Why does the wind keep doing this to me?' Junior moaned. His hands were under his chin now, clasped in prayer.

It seemed to him there was an awkwardness about the Phantom's turn, as if it were doing something it didn't want to do, as if it were resisting. Then the Phantom began moving towards them. Junior knew that the last time it had done this it had kept right on moving until it got to old man Benson's chicken house.

He spun around. 'Mom, it's going to the chicken house again.'

'Maybe not, hon,' his mother said. 'Anyway, don't worry about that, I can handle old man Benson. Just don't let yourself get upset.'

'I'm trying not to,' Junior wailed.

Another breeze started up the hill, Junior could hear the leaves rustling. The new breeze caused the Phantom to bob in the air and shift courses again.

It seemed to Junior then that all the different winds in the world were struggling with his Phantom, trying to send it where he most didn't want it to go.

'Where's it going now? What's happening? Where's it going?'

Junior looked around for the place he most didn't want it to go, because he knew from past experience that would most likely be the Phantom's destination.

He saw it immediately—the oak tree. The Phantom was directly over their heads, and it was on a straight path for the oak tree.

The only thing that could save it now was another breeze. 'Come on, breeze, come on, breeze,' Junior began to mutter under his breath. 'Come on, breeze.'

He stood there helpless, tears rolling unchecked down his cheeks, hands clasped in prayer, and watched his precious Phantom move closer and closer to disaster.

'That stupid wind,' Maggie muttered. 'It just can't land in the tree. It can't.'

Ralphie did not want to be the one to

tell her that it not only could, but it was going to.

Even though Junior knew the worst, he was not prepared for how terrible he would feel when it happened. The sounds were so sad. Plastic brushing against leaves, catching on twigs, then that fatal silken sigh he had come to know, and then silence.

For a long moment nobody spoke. Maybe everybody felt as he did, Junior thought, that as long as nobody said anything, it wouldn't really have happened. The Phantom would break away and keep going. The moment stretched on, but this didn't happen. The Phantom remained where it was, a beautiful unearthly blob, glowing against the darker foliage of the tree.

And what made it so especially terrible, Junior thought, was that he would have to look at this sight for the rest of his life. He could see this tree from the road. He would have to watch the Phantom deteriorate, the way he had watched his American flag-kite fade and shred and die on the electrical wires across the road. He would have to watch the polka dots fade, and the garbage bags tatter. He would have to watch the air mattresses grow limp and—

Junior's shoulders sagged and his mom came over and put her arm around him. 'It looks like it's stuck, hon, but it was very beautiful while it lasted. I just loved it. Everybody did.'

Junior pulled away. He said what he knew all along he would have to say. 'If I can climb up on a chicken house to save it, I can climb a plain old tree.'

And with his head high, Junior started walking.

IN THE TREE WITH MAGGIE

'Junior, you are not climbing that tree.'

'Let me go! Let me go!'

Junior's mother spun him around. She had him by both arms, but Junior kept twisting as hard as he could. His mother held on as hard as she could. Junior realized that if his mother had been holding him that night at old man

151

Benson's farm, he would not have ended up on the chicken house.

'I said to let me go!' He gave a final desperate twist. Still his mother held him.

'Listen to me. I will let you go when you calm down and not a minute sooner.'

Junior stopped struggling. He stood there, looking down at the ground, breathing hard. Then he threw one agonized glance up at the Phantom.

'Junior.' His mother's voice forced him to look back at her. 'Junior, the reason you are not going to climb that tree is because if you fall and break those legs again, you will be crippled for the rest of your life. Nothing is worth that.'

'I'll be glad to do it, Mrs Blossom,' Ralphie said.

She turned to look at him. 'But you have a bad leg too, don't you, Ralphie?'

'Yes, but that doesn't stop me from doing anything I want to do.' Then he said what he believed to be the truth. 'If anybody can get it down, I can.'

'I'll help,' Maggie said quickly.

Ralphie drew in his breath, taken completely by surprise at Maggie's offer. He had offered to climb the tree because offering to do things for Junior had become almost a way of life. The thought that Maggie might climb with him had never even crossed his mind.

'Will you two be very careful?' Vicki Blossom asked.

'Yes,' Ralphie answered.

'Michael and I will help too.'

Ralphie's delight in climbing a tree with Maggie dimmed at the thought of taking along her brother and his friend.

'No, thanks, Vern,' Ralphie said quickly, 'it's a two-man job. Mrs Blossom, if we get too many people up there somebody might fall. I couldn't be responsible.'

'Vern, you and Michael stay down here.' It was a Blossom order, and Ralphie sighed with quick relief.

'We'll give you a boost.' Michael and Vern were already at the tree with their hands clasped together. Now that Junior saw those clasped hands, he was glad someone else was going to be boosted up this time.

Maggie got the first boost, then Ralphie. 'Wait!' Mad Mary said. Everyone was so shocked to hear her actually say something that they stopped what they were doing.

Mad Mary crossed to the tree with long strides. 'Here,' she said, 'maybe this will help.'

She passed up her long cane with the crook on the end. Maggie took it. 'Why, thank you.'

Then she handed it to Ralphie. 'Thank you,' he said. He reached up and hooked it over an upper branch. 'Let's go.'

Ralphie was good in trees. Sometimes he even took off his leg to prove just how good he was, but obviously this was not the time to show off.

He got up the first two branches like a shot so that he could lean down and offer his hand to Maggie. She took it. He glanced up. Ah, about ten more branches, twelve if he went the hard way, twelve more offers of help. Ralphie hooked Mad Mary's cane over the next branch and moved up.

'Mud, stop that,' Pap said, 'let Dump go.'

Now that Maggie and Ralphie were out of sight in the tree, Pap had looked down. He did this mainly to give his neck muscles a rest, but the first thing he saw was Mud, holding Dump down on the ground with his paw.

'Stop it, Mud.'

Mud took his paw off Dump, and Dump ran to Pap. He put his thin paws on Pap's knee. Pap leaned down and scratched him behind the ears. 'You ought to be ashamed of yourself, Mud.'

Mud's ears pulled back. His tail went between his legs.

'I been noticing how you been carrying on. You won't let the puppy drink water out of your bowl and you won't let him eat at all and now you won't let him walk around. What's wrong with you?'

Mud hung his head.

'Just go on,' Pap said. 'Go on. If you can't behave yourself, Mud, just go on back to the house.'

Mud took a few steps away from the people, towards the path where Pap was pointing.

'We'll be glad to have your company if you can behave yourself, but if you can't, just go on. I'm tired of watching you make this puppy's life miserable.'

Mud went a few more steps. He sat down. He watched Pap patting the puppy. He waited for a long time for Pap to speak to him and tell him things were all right. When he didn't, Mud turned and with his tail between his legs, he started for home.

*   *   *

Maggie was a good climber too, but that didn't surprise Ralphie. He knew himself well enough to know he would never fall in love with a girl who was clumsy.

They got up to the level of the Phantom too quickly to suit Ralphie, and he had only himself to blame. He was in such a hurry for the next handhold, that he didn't let the

156

individual holds last long enough. What he should have done was—

Maggie broke into his thoughts. 'Do you want to crawl out on that branch or this one?'

'I'll take the one you don't want,' he said graciously.

'I'll go out on this one. I weigh less and . . . ' She grinned and he could see her broken tooth up close for the first time. It was much more beautiful up close. It was like—he was sorry he wasn't a more poetic person because it wasn't like anything really except Maggie's tooth. It was his favourite of her teeth, of course, but it was like nothing in the world but her tooth. He hardly heard the end of her sentence, ' . . . since it's the smallest . . . '

Junior called from the ground, 'Are you there yet?'

'We're there,' Maggie called back.

'Can you reach it?'

'Give us time,' Ralphie answered.

They inched out on their branches and stopped when they were directly below the branch that held the Phantom. Ralphie reached out with

157

Mad Mary's cane and poked it. 'It's going to take more than this. Let's shake.'

Maggie nodded. They reached up together and grabbed the branch. 'Ready?' Ralphie asked.

Maggie nodded. Then she added, 'Wait a minute, let me get a better grip.'

'Me too,' Ralphie said.

Maggie really wanted a better grip, but Ralphie just wanted a way to make the time in the tree with Maggie last longer. He wondered if all men loved women more in trees than they did on the ground, or if it was just him. Maybe it was the way the moonlight shone through the leaves on her face. Or maybe it ws the fact that they seemed so much more alone at this moment than they had ever been before.

'I'm ready,' she said.

'Okay,' Ralphie said. 'Go!'

They both began to shake, and it was one of the most exciting moments of Ralphie's life. Maggie was laughing and leaves and twigs were falling all around them.

Maggie stretched forward and looked up. 'It's still there. Go again!'

They shook harder this time. Leaves and twigs rained around them. Maggie laughed aloud.

Then she leaned forward to look.

'It's free,' she cried. 'It's free!'

She had to keep leaning forward to watch the Phantom's escape. Ralphie could see all right from where he was, but he found himself leaning forward too.

Instead of looking up at the Phantom, however, he looked down at Maggie's face. Her eyes were shining. Her lips were smiling.

And to Ralphie's amazement he bent his head and kissed her.

GOING . . . GOING . . . GONE

'Can you see it all right up there?' Junior yelled. 'Can you guys see it?'

Ralphie tried to make his voice normal when he called back, 'Yes.'

'It's so beautiful,' Junior went on in

159

an excited way, 'and the breeze is just right. Come on down quick so you see it.'

'We can see real good from up here, Junior,' Maggie called back.

She looked down as she called to Junior, and all Ralphie could see was the top of her head, her centre parting, the braids swinging on either side of her face. She did not sound like a girl who had just been kissed. She sounded perfectly normal.

Ralphie knew that the one word he had managed had not sounded normal at all. He knew, too, that he did not look normal either. His face was on fire. The tips of his ears blazed.

Maggie glanced up at him then and grinned. She did not look like a girl who had just been kissed either. It was exactly the same friendly grin she always gave him.

'Can you see all right?' she asked.

'Yes.'

'How do you know? You aren't even looking.'

'Oh.' Ralphie actually looked through the leaves at the Phantom for the first time.

The Phantom was moving away on the wind, over the cliff, over the tallest trees, soaring towards the city of Alderson. 'Wouldn't it be funny,' Maggie said, 'if people saw it and thought it was real?'

Ralphie still didn't trust his voice to say more than one word at a time. 'Yes.'

'Wouldn't it be great if it got in the newspaper. UFO Sighted Over Alderson. Junior would be so thrilled.'

Ralphie cleared his throat. 'He seems pretty thrilled as it is.'

'I know. I just think I would have died if it had gone wrong tonight. Last night was terrible. Last night was one of the worst nights of my life. You heard the things Mom said to me.'

Ralphie cleared his throat. 'But tonight's been all right, hasn't it?'

'Yes.'

'On a scale of one to ten, how would you rate it?'

'Oh.' She thought a minute. 'Ten.' Her answer thrilled him so much, he would have fallen out of the tree if he hadn't been hooked on to a branch by Mad Mary's cane.

'If you don't watch out, Ralphie, you're going to fall and ruin the whole thing.'

Ralphie regained his balance quickly. After that he pretended to watch the Phantom, but the Phantom was nothing compared to Maggie. He watched Maggie out of the sides of his eyes.

'We'd better start down,' Maggie said. 'I promised Mom I'd do the refreshments. We're having two flavours of Kool-Aid, pimento cheese sandwiches, and Oreos.'

Ralphie said, 'What's the hurry? Nobody will want to eat until the Phantom's out of sight anyway.'

Maggie looked up at the sky and grinned. 'It is out of sight.'

And before he could stop her, Maggie swung to the next lower branch and began climbing down. Even he couldn't have done it so fast. With a sigh, he unhooked Mad Mary's cane and started after her.

★   ★   ★

Below, on the ground, Junior said, 'Wasn't it just beautiful, wasn't it beautiful? I think I can still see it, can you, Mom?'

'Maybe,' his mother said. She couldn't, but she knew that Junior might still be seeing it in his mind, and she didn't want to disturb the image.

Junior was seeing it in his mind, replaying it the way things were replayed on television. He was not replaying the whole thing. He started his motion with the Phantom breaking away from the tree. That had been the most spectacular part.

There had been a burst of leaves and twigs as if the Phantom itself were trying to pull free, and then it was free. It was in the air. It paused for a moment, and then immediately it began to gain height. It seemed to shoot straight up, more like a rocket than a balloon. And in five minutes the Phantom had actually become a part of the sky, something that had always belonged there, like the sun or the moon. It was as if he, Junior, had

163

released the Phantom from captivity, and put it where it was meant to be.

'I wish everybody in the world could see it,' Junior said.

'Maybe they will,' his mom answered.

The Green Phantom, Junior thought, is my gift to the world.

Vern said, 'Well, I can't see it, can you, Michael?'

Michael said, 'No.'

There was such regret in Michael's voice that Vern glanced at him. It was the same regret he felt over not playing with the BB gun or the rod and reel. He felt a warmth towards Michael that for the first time had nothing to do with Michael's possessions.

'Wait a minute,' Vicki Blossom said, 'maybe you can't see it, but Junior's got better eyes than the rest of the family.'

This time when Junior looked it was gone. 'No,' he said, 'it's gone out into the world.'

His mother took his hand, and they walked to where Maggie was spreading out the night picnic. Actually, it wasn't like walking, Junior thought, it was more pleasant than that. It was strolling.

'Did you really like it, Mom?' he asked on the way.

'I loved it. You know what it reminded me of?'

'What?'

'The Fourth of July, only it was even better than fireworks.'

Since Junior dearly loved fireworks, this pleased him. He stopped strolling for a moment. His mother did too. 'What is it, Junior?'

'If I ask you something, will you tell me the truth?'

'Of course.'

Junior had to ask this while the Phantom was still in his mother's mind. This was the most important question of Junior's life.

'Do you think Dad would have been proud of me?'

'Oh, yes,' his mother answered. And she repeated it so Junior knew she really did mean it. 'Oh, yes.'

THE MISERY HOLE

Mud was under the porch when the Blossom family came home from the launch. He rolled his eyes upwards as they climbed the porch steps above him and a little dust sprinkled down through the floorboards. Mud did not lift his head. He was too miserable.

He heard the family cross the porch, open the door, go into the house. He heard the light steps of the puppy going in with them. He heard the excitement in the Blossoms' voices as they got ready for bed.

'What was your favourite part, Maggie?'

'My favourite part, Junior, was when the Phantom broke out of the tree.'

'Mom, what was your favourite part?'

'Let's see. I have so many favourites. But I think my very favourite was towards the end when the Phantom sort of blended in with the stars.'

'Pap, what was your very favourite

part?'

'Getting home.'

Mud's ear twitched when he heard Pap's voice, but he kept his body curled into a ball, his head resting on his paws, his tail tucked between his legs. From time to time his body trembled.

This was Mud's misery hole, and it perfectly fitted his body. He had made it over the years and he got in it every time Pap fussed at him or wanted to give him a bath or left him behind, but he had never needed it more than he did now. The worst thing in his life had happened. Pap had gotten a new dog.

The porch light went out and the little slits of light that had filtered through the cracks between the boards were gone. Mud was in darkness. He sighed and trembled. He felt worse than ever. As long as the light had been on, there had been a chance that Pap would open the door and call him inside. Now the house was silent. No one was going to call.

Mud stood his misery as long as he could. Then he lifted his head and began to howl softly. It wasn't his usual howl. His usual howl could be heard for five miles. This was a wail of such sorrow that it barely penetrated the floorboards of the Blossoms' house.

Pap was the one who heard it. 'Oh, I forgot about Mud.' He threw back his covers and got out of bed. He went down the hall, through the dark living room, and threw open the porch door. He turned on the light.

'Mud, are you under the porch?'

Mud stopped howling. There was a silence.

'Mud, are you under the porch?'

Silence.

Mud heard Pap's feet on the porch, crossing to the steps. Pap went down one step and stopped.

'Come on out, boy. Come on, Mud.'

Mud did not move. Pap said, 'Now don't make me come all the way down the steps and get down on my knees and pull you out. You know what my knees are like.'

Pap waited. Then he sighed. He went down the stairs slowly and bent to peer under the house. Mud was there where Pap knew he would be—in his misery hole.

'Come on out, Mud, good dog. Come on.'

Mud did not move.

'Mud, don't make me come in there after you.'

Still Mud did not move.

Pap sighed. Then he lay down on his stomach and worked his way under the house. He reached out one trembling hand and laid it on top of Mud's head. He began to smooth the wrinkles in Mud's brow with his thumb.

'Now, you know I don't stay mad with you, don't you? I'm already over it. You know that. You're the best dog I ever had, Mud, and lately maybe I haven't been acting like I appreciate you, but I do. I surely do.'

He kept smoothing Mud's brow. 'There's never been a better dog than you. This new dog—he's a nice little dog, but he ain't mine. I'm like my daddy when it comes to dogs. My daddy used to keep the fine dogs for himself and give ordinary dogs to us kids. Like he kept Old Stoker for himself and gave me Little Blackie, and

Little Blackie chased chickens. My mama was always after me about that. I'd say, 'Mama, he don't catch them,' but every time she'd see him, he'd be grinning and there'd be a chicken feather stuck on his tongue. You're my dog like Old Stoker was my daddy's. I don't need another dog. I wouldn't take one if somebody gave it to me. I'm a one-dog man, and you're a one-man dog. We belong together. Now come on out. You can sleep under my bed if you want to. Come on, Mud. Please let's get up off this hard ground.'

He twisted his fingers in the bandanna that Mud wore around his neck. He pulled, and Mud slid out of his misery hole.

'Now you know you don't want to spend the night under the porch, come on. You and me have been through too much to let one little disagreement ruin things. Come on.'

Mud's tail thumped once against the porch steps. 'That's my dog, come on. Let's go, Mud.'

Mud crawled out from under the porch. He sat and waited patiently for

Pap to crawl out too.

Pap didn't get up right away. He lay on his back for a moment, catching his breath. And then he did something he had never done before. He put his arms around Mud and hugged him against his chest.

'There's too few living beings in this world that I care about for me to go around treating one of them the way I treated you. You forgive Pap this time, and I won't make the same mistake again.'

Pap released Mud and began the long struggle to his feet. Mud shook himself while he waited. Then Pap said, 'Come on, Mud, let's go to bed.' And Mud followed Pap into the house.

THE FINISH

It was one week later, and every one of the Blossoms had something to be pleased about. Maggie had caught on to standing up in shortened stirrups and could now go around the field on Sandy

Boy almost as fast as her mom.

'Watch, Ralphie!' she called, even though she was aware Ralphie had not taken his eyes off her since he got there.

Ralphie was lying on the grass. He was smiling slightly. Ralphie had something to be pleased about too. His mother had found out about the helium, and she had not clobbered him. Of course, this was, Ralphie told himself, because he had been sharp enough to say, 'Mom, even hardened criminals get to atone for their crimes.'

'And just how are you planning to atone?'

'I'll help deliver balloons, Mom. This gorilla woman can't last. People want balloons delivered by clowns. You need a clown suit. Mom, the whole family could be clowns. I could be a pirate clown with a peg leg.'

Ralphie hoped he would not actually have to be a peg-leg clown, but it had diverted his mom, and she had gone this afternoon to look at patterns for clown suits.

Vicki Blossom was pleased because in the spring, she would be back on the rodeo circuit, this time with Maggie. She could almost hear the announcer saying, 'And joining the Wrangler Riders is a three-generation cowgirl. Her grandad is Pap Blossom. Her dad was Cotton Blossom, a National Champion, and that's her proud mom, Vicki Blossom. Let's put our hands together and give all the Blossoms, past and present, a round of applause.'

Pap was pleased because he was getting ready to show Vern how to wash a dog. He felt he had a special knack for washing dogs. 'You don't wash them like people,' was the way he described his technique. 'Come on, Dump, you need a bath.'

Mud heard the word *bath*, and he slipped under the porch. He kept his body low so he would not call attention to himself. He hid behind the steps in his misery hole. He waited.

The usual procedure was that Pap would say the word *bath*, then call Mud and remove his bandanna. Mud hated to have his bandanna removed. It gave him an unprotected feeling. But this time Pap headed down to the creek with Dump under one arm. Mud crawled out to see what was happening.

Vern had the bucket with the soap and towels in it. 'Junior,' Vern called, 'are you coming?'

Junior had insisted on washing his half of the dog himself. 'Five minutes,' he pleaded from the kitchen.

'Well, hurry, I've got to go to Michael's.'

'I'm hurrying as fast as I can.'

Junior was sitting at the kitchen table, smiling at the refrigerator. Five minutes before, he had been smiling at the sink, then at the stove. Junior shook himself. He looked down at the sheet of paper in front of him and forced his face to be serious.

He smiled again. He couldn't help it. Every time he thought about the Phantom, he smiled.

As long as Junior lived, he would never forget that night last week, when the Phantom had very quietly, very naturally, taken its place in the sky and begun its circle around the world. When he thought of it, he had even begun to hear background music—

violins mostly, but also there were some flutes in it too.

All week he had followed in his mind the global orbit of the Phantom. He had imagined it over the burning Sahara, over the white icy Arctic, over the Atlantic, the Pacific, Russia, China.

Junior stopped smiling at the sheet of paper. He made himself look serious. He had to finish this. He had to.

He read the words to himself. 'I want to win a trip around the world for my entire family because—'

That was the same place where his mind always stopped working. It was as if his mind had heard a bell ringing and rushed out to recess. He knocked on his forehead to activate his brain.

'I want to win a trip around the world for my entire family because—'

The reason he did want to win was hard to put into words. Last week, at the peak of his Phantom success, he had realized how much he loved his family. He loved them so much that he wanted to do something for them as nice as they had done for him.

And what could be better than

winning a trip for them, the same trip that the Phantom was now making? Junior was going to win a trip around the world for his family. He would write the winning sentence today, and then he would save it until a contest came along, and then he would copy the sentence onto the blank.

He bent over his paper. He was absolutely determined. His mouth was a straight line in his round face.

'I want to win a trip around the world for my entire family because—'

He lifted his head in sudden thought.

Maggie had said something that made sense one time. It was when Junior and Ralphie had been in the hospital, and Ralphie had asked Maggie why they broke into the city gaol, why they didn't just walk in like anybody else.

And Maggie had looked at Ralphie like he didn't have good sense. 'We Blossoms,' she said, 'have never been just anybody.'

'Junior, you coming?' Vern called.

'Yes, don't let my half get wet!'

'Well, hurry!'

'I am hurrying!'

He bent over his paper. He clicked his ballpoint pen open. He began to write.

He smiled. Maggie and their mom might be on the rodeo circuit next summer, but the rest of them—Vern and Pap and he and Mud and Dump—would very definitely be going around the world.

'I want to win a trip around the world for my entire family because we Blossoms have never been just anybody.' He paused for a moment because, as usual, he wanted to add his own personal touch. Again, he smiled. He changed his period to a comma and added, 'and we never will be either.'

Junior put an exclamation point and laid down his pen. He was finished at last. He folded the sheet of paper, put it in his shirt pocket, and patted it. Then he got up and ran for the door.

'I'm coming!' he cried.

Photoset, printed and bound in Great Britain by REDWOOD BURN LIMITED, Trowbridge, Wiltshire